BREATH LIKE THE WIND AT DAWN

DEVIN JACOBSEN

Sagging
Meniscus

A portion of this work first appeared in *Hobart*.

Printed in the United States of America.
Set in Williams Caslon Text with LATEX.

ISBN: 978-1-944697-93-8 (paperback)
ISBN: 978-1-944697-81-5 (ebook)
Library of Congress Control Number: 2019952095

Sagging Meniscus Press
Montclair, New Jersey
saggingmeniscus.com

BREATH
LIKE
THE
WIND
AT
DAWN

1

Yonder they lay: a tangle the like of fleas. They that we had
sought since long before sunup this morning hovered a bit
and sank from the horizon. Quinn and I had been jogging;
now looking together, loping of a sudden to reclaim the
distance, we raced to where they set.

The sky shot through with clouds, dusky like patterned
roses. I feel myself become all entity with the horses. That
instant when horse and man and tack float up a single
being—cinches, hooves, and stomachs waiting there—the
suspension—and then that beat where you are sundered,
jolted into knowing that you have merged and been torn
apart, only to do so again the next moment, because the
horse carrying out your purpose has done the job so well it
is as though you have fulfilled the feat yourself. You hover
there like that as much a horse as man.

I recall once watching a Saddlebred pass a gelding who
was walking a lazy walk and thinking something was funny,
off. No simple difference of appearance. Something fundamentally at odds in the two horses' natures that watching's
abetting could not enlighten.

I studied the Saddlebred jogging by, one beside the
other. Nothing unusual, a sight seen every day by all likes
and types of folks and everywhere, but in this passing was
something wholly different.

As I came to sift it, I perceived first by the noise of the
jogger against the walker (it required a new way of seeing
since seeing would not behold). Only by letting my eyes,

trained on them, the passer's thighs and form at large, go loose yet still implacable could I behold it: the feet moving in apparent twos, in tandem diagonals, so unlike the walker's whose plodded one leg at a time, one behind and then in front, this side followed by that. They were walking two different walks.

And a canter has got a different gait from a jog, which has a different gait from a walk, which has a different gait from a gallop.

Once I saw a man stride his horse so high his fetlocks reached his muzzle. Round and round they went, cavorting, a hilarious smile so wide an eagle's nest could fit inside. Tipping his hat to the bewildered applause.

Whether he or someone else had trained the mare to prance that way he would not say despite my plying. So I beat him and stole his horse.

2

Watching the smoke of the unsighted fire, they waited for the noon of night to come, and once it had they began to lurk forward, up the rise, where they waited for the fire to grow dark. The smoke, nearly unreal like a defect of the eye that stays forever tagging the viewer, extinguished among the myriad stars.

Laughter broke. A loud wind shook the camp so that the smoke appeared to have died altogether. Voices slurred, of which there were nine. Then the wind went off, and for a moment the night lay taut with silence.

Soon the foodsmell in the air. They heard utensils pecking at pans, the while fixed on the trailing smoke.

"Let's go bust em. Tell em we're here for supper."

"No. They need to get more drunk."

"There won't be gristle left in them pans."

"Hawk them Pepperboxes. You'll eat like a king for a week."

"I'll take my king on an empty stomach, thank you."

"Shhh."

They stayed against the rise, where they listened to the voices begin to pitch louder. Trying not to move or fend off what felt like ticks crawling around their thighs or laugh when someone said something dumb.

At one point one of them rose. Kicking a path through the brush, he came near to alighting on them. The liquid running down, conjuring up leaves and dust and motes and casting them down on its flood. Paralyzed, they held there beyond the draw. They could hear the grass lift off the ground as it rushed and went.

The stranger hawked into the dark, though neglecting his buckle—Quinn making to chime, Irv reining him no— and turned and went.

"Let me tell you boys about kidding and why I don't." His melodious, quavering voice becoming the voice of night. "A fella can't afford to play no games. He can't play nothing but keeping his wheels in line. Ain't that what a man is? His seriousness like to defines him. He ain't a boy can tool around the way he used to, pulling pranks. No, his absence of a fool defines him.

"Let me tell you boys. I rode of a company with a trick-ster, a drafty door of a fellow who pulled more pranks than pulled his pecker, and when we was coming back, not a half-day's ride from his hometown, he catches wind his ma and sister have set to running a little inn. With the farm pretty much all sold they was pretty hard up for cash and took to running a little inn where there was always some fella about they could count on for protection.

"So the trickster borrows a coat, a big old gus and wears her low, and rents himself a room at his own mama's inn where she and the sister don't much recognize him, the brother, the trickster, who is spouting off in a Yankee tongue about how much cash he raked up manufacturing Union rifles and how much he aims to surprise his own ma and sister when he sees them flush with cash a few days hence, and everyone's a load of laughs.

"Then he bids them goodnight, tucks himself abed, snuffs his candle, and commences to fall asleep. In the morning he's gonna reveal himself and tell them how it was all just a joke. But that's the trouble with pulling pranks:

you can't be sharp thinking you're the only trickster. You get to fooling yourself you're the only joker in the deck.

"Well, our fella gets abed, and during the night the mother and sister slip in, and before he can say, 'How do,' they slit his throat from ear to ear and clean out every one of his coat pockets and take what cash he's holding. Next morning after the sun comes up and the guests have all gone home, they go on back to clear the room, and what do they see in that bed, only the trickster, the boy, the son. Mother goes crazy and drowns herself; sister eats poison. And that's why I don't kid."

They heard the fire collapse and saw the sparks burn out among the stars.

"What about the daddy?" said one.

"Why the daddy came home a happy man!"

Laughter erupted through the camp.

After a while they began to dwindle, and what had been a cluster of voices became a selection of four identities drifting on a tide of snoring. The smoke from the campfire now vague, intermittent. Periodic howling cleft the dark.

"Don't want to make it too easy," said Quinn.

"Right," said Irving. He took out his Remington and cocked her.

Doffing their hats, they shifted up farther, up to the extreme ledge, until they could venture a judicious glance. About thirty paces yonder were the men sprawled out like a den of cats. Some had fallen asleep with their rifles on their chests, their feet upturned to the warmth. Beyond the ring the eyes of horses, small points of fire, as if someone had gone and thrown gems into the night.

Quinn shivered, then Irving.

"I'ma go for a waker," said Quinn. At that he licked his lips.

They each took aim, sharing a grin. Made the silent countdown.

Gusts emerged from their guns. Shouts spilled forth instantaneous; as the men went for their arms, they were effectively felled back. Something inside them seemed to snap, go off, go wrong, as random body parts ejaculated blood. The embers hissed, doused in blood. Those who did fire appeared to be discharging at an abstract sense of retaliation, one sending a shot that seemed cast in multiple directions at once.

Within half a minute most were splayed and dead. A few were moaning, thrashing by the dark fire when the twins crested the rise.

Their hands blackened and holding full cylinders, they surveyed the camp.

Irv worked the circle, giving each an ensuring bullet: their faces blossomed with shot. Noting a set of rowels he'd come back for. A sizeable Whitney with ivory grips.

"This one pissed hisself."

"Where?" yelled Quinn.

"Wait!" he heard. "Don't shoot!"

"Why not?" said Irving. He said this without criticizing, as if he just wanted to know.

"What's this?" Quinn said. He trotted over. He was hugging more guns than he could carry.

"I don't know," he told him. "You get your pistols?"

From his hips he flashed the Pepperbox Derringers, the pure gelid silver of them shining to polished sickles.

"Damn," he said on making his inspection of the boy, a corpse not half alive. "Fella's sure had hisself a beating. Ain't a cheery day, is it, pal?"

"Please," he said, "don't kill me."

The fellow had been much shot. Something of a hand lay at his side, which had been more or less blown off from the wrist, and the tips of the fingers were continuing to move, catching the light.

"What in the *hel*-pful doctor happened to you?"

In the tampered embers he found the culprit: a Root Revolving Rifle washed with powder. Irv came, bearing a lantern.

"Whoowee," hollered Quinn. "I'd say you had yourself a chain fire! That's why you always gotta grease her, otherwise she's bound to go off. I'd say you shot your load all at once you done. Shot her right into your hand."

He looked a terrible discarded version of humanoid, some entity painful to look at.

"Please, wait," he said, his breath tremulous and weak. "I can make it worth your while."

"Oh," said Irving, "how's that?"

Grimacing, he strained, readying to speak. Instead his legs jerked out from under him, which caused a startled Quinn to jump back, tripping back, guns and everything.

Then there were two of them hurt on the ground. Irv seized the occasion to laugh until he realized his brother's eye had fallen out. It had just plopped out and was waggling against his lips. Its unraveled exposure nearly indecent, evoking the visual shock of a private part.

"Put it back! Put it back!" he was screaming. Shouting, flailing, a madman.

"Okay. Okay! I can't if you keep fighting me!"

He brought the light close and propped it on a corpse. After ushering his twin to kneel, he spread his eyelids open, finger and thumb. Gazing into the chasm as one would peer into another's brain and attempt to read his thoughts. But the light did not quite reach and Quinn was yelling too hard, so that the most he could gather of such an insight was a dank and curious wetness.

With the other hand he plucked up the dangling eyeball, winding the thread into the socket, deftly, like a competitor in a game pressed for time, but paused to regard his brother's eye—stared at the moist red ball—because in a way it was something he had never quite seen despite gazing at his whole life, which he then popped back with his thumb. Quinn swore fiercely.

He returned to the boy with the shot-off hand. Again he cocked his pistol.

"Wait!" he cried once more.

"No," said Irving, his humor that of a lifter strained beyond his capacity, "you shut up now."

"But there's gold," he said.

He could hear him quivering.

"Gold." He hesitated, paused. Even to utter the word contained an element of testing, and because of this he repeated, "Gold," this time feeling it faintly real.

"Where?" he said. His manner shifty, he shone the lantern against him so that all he could see was light.

"Utica Bank. They's plenty. More than you can fit to think. The safe, my daddy—"

"Utica? Where the hell is Utica? How come I ain't never heard of no Utica before?"

The boy lay there with all the wanting to run, but with a body that cannot.

"Bout ninety miles west of Mankato. Please," he said, "just please, please don't kill me, sir."

A hand mashed against his socket, Quinn lumbered forward, his good eye glowering. He pointed a weary gun.

"Shoot, I oughta skin you alive for tripping me," he told him, kicking him until he had raised a squeally uproar. He fired a shot over his head at the dark. Then they heard a horse go squealing in the dark. Irv steadied an arm on his twin's.

"Hold just a second. How do I know that you ain't lying?"

The boy wanted to take deep breaths, but all he could do was try. His teeth were lost in a mess the length of his shirt that made a quilt of blooming wet patches.

"My daddy, he was the builder. He built the Utica Bank."

"Good for him," said Quinn. He hefted the pistol. "Time to die."

"No!" His youthful voice did not at all match his miserable appearance. "Wait, I mean there's a cave! Bout two miles east of the town. In the back of a little barn looks like a gingerbread. Near the bottom of the hill. My daddy, he built her atop a X way down in that cave. You dig up through that X you're in the vault. I'll show you. Just please, please don't kill me, sir."

Irv cocked his pistol and watched as his face exploded, Quinn following suit. They emptied the remains of their cylinders into the unbecoming figure, into the ruining face.

Powder hovered about the camp, an eerie pall, as if they two had concluded some necromantic rites, though leaving the conjured spirits remote to find their way home. Both of them standing there frozen.

"Shoot," Quinn said. "You think anybody heard?"

"Let's just go and bag it," said Irving.

Ignoring a Springfield and Jenks carbine, they rounded up the others: an imposing LeMat, a muskatoon, the typical pistols.

While they were going to pony the horses they noticed that one had been accidently shot. The horse, an Appaloosa dappled from the croup, was wobbling and heaving, her ears tucked flat against her skull, oblivious to their orders. Irv undid her halter, and they watched as she, as though forced by a special magnetism, drifted back to the tree. There she continued to moan, banging her head against the trunk.

They stayed for a while, the two of them watching her shiver and twitch at the cold.

3

It is of night. Since in day he ain't to rest, and in night he ain't to sleep. There is the waiting and the quiet and the wanting him to come.

She feels it coming, to look in at through the window. Out there amongst the dark and trees and stars and the hanging of a maid and them souls wandering out over the plain. And him a-coming to wait at what he wants, since to wait is a kind of faith. To keep you here in arms.

Wait! he stares her. Wait! Since to wait is a kind of faith and the faith a babe, a babe waiting to burst ope. Always yonder out over the plain. Since knowing is to work his want and take you to her breast. Going adrift out over the plain. To lead a dame to bed.

In day he ain't to rest, but in night he ain't to sleep, since in night he seeks to come. It is of night, round noon of dark, with all save the faith asleep, just knowing and waiting and wanting, alone as a body in her grave, only the thing adrift in her thoughts, who keeps to the patch of moonglow, now to wink and feel your touch, to feel your figure at looking in, out there amongst the faith and trees and stars. To take you here in arms.

It is a face made old and young. The face an old, old man turned back to first-dayed babe, or a babe grown to last day, a face shorn of any feature, who ain't eyed nor nosed nor eared. And skin so frail like a hand-me-down or some bobbin-net too rich for use. You hover there, stayed at looking in. It is a lone sad quiet hunger from a pain that only a body can know. For his look goes jerking and jib-bering cause he's past talk, for he ain't yet to hold his love compan.

Since he catches of her a look. Stayed at looking in. Alone as a body in grave. And she is got up abed to wel-come you to the door with a kind of a touch, a welcome-back loving-clinging, an offering of blood. So fair she is and young and ready in hope to begin the journey, since she must work to do your bid, to whisper vows. Yet hold-ing till you allow it so.

Open the door, round the bend, relieved to see you ungone. Wandered out yet over the plain, if but to keep you here in arms. He is of nightclothes and aglow. Some-thing trembling with awe and moon, always angling for his dame; he comes to court, woo, beckoning, beckoning love. For someone to feed your stare to man, to keep you here in arms.

They go, lovers as much as drifting, adrift out over the plain, since the nearer she is drawn the nearer the heavens ope. He is of a right tired hungry spirit. One seeking, the other sought. And so she begins to run. Yet at seeing him to hold, afeard her haste's to spook, her feet forget to want, love compan and wife.

Over the rill, the water glad, awake, a girl up in her mind. And him adrift, peering at, peering down, his mouth agog in hate and blankless stare who ain't yet eared nor eyed nor nosed. Since he ain't to stare but in a blameful way, and her, alag, gain up, for his stare is of night and hate. It is a fiery kind of hate, a yelling-back loving hate, since she's to blame, alag. In his hollow without any tongue, he screams for her to run. Then gone behind the verge.

Curses a-buzzing over the air, working to bringing them home, if but to keep you here in arms. She hastes, but so's not to frighten, since the nearer she is drawn the nearer the heavens ope. Then when she tops, he holds his stay, cursing his way yonder. Hovering there and waiting, for her to work his bid. Then yonder they continue to go.

Under a sky pained with light, she stabs her spade. Stooped, hoping to dare a glimpse. She is a dame to know you for afeard of day. That though you ain't near, yet you are by, and the faith inside a-growing, waiting at what it wants. So day is the same as night, and your glow to prove her worth.

Sailing down hills, past neighbor farms. Shadowy stones of cows asleep or dead in prayer. They skirt them, shapeless as a loaf.

On nearing the den of beech, there is the tale of Lilian, fair maid. Wooed by the shade of her love compan, who hunted him through the pine, never seen by her tribe of Santee, and gone the days of love. Only my figure's for a true. We go, never nearer as we are far, our love a fire without any top.

If only he'd let her take him, keep you here in arms, nurse him, give him strength. His linen soaking, dripping with blood, to become the man he must, and all the strength yet waiting, wanting, dripping with blood, since he ain't yet eyed nor eared nor nosed and hollow without any tongue. It is of a warmth and a first-dayed babe, his shade thickening to face, face roughed to person, quicked in sucks of blood.

It is of a bird afeard who won't let you touch him, who aims to fly away, and when you hold him in your palm you feel his heart abeat, the thing there poor and trembling. If but to catch him here in arms, if but to bear him on the verge, to nurse him on her blood, since what pain it is to go, always yonder out over the plain, since she must work to do your bid.

Staying, so does he. For fear she blink and lest them spirits point their fingers, she stirs, to move on still. In lending you this skin he knows she's good to work. Yet in the light come up she sees this place for her pain of days, a trick to watch her hopes soon flare as quench, but if he is cruel, it is a cruel for her own must.

She is wrong, for you are thinning? If but to keep you here in arms. The two of them stopped, she begs you stay, if for the sake of not to go, for since she's to blame if these old feet couldn't race to win, but only weening yonder, love. He goes a-hovering and a-listening. Stay, she begs him. Please. If but to punish, your beats the tenders of a hand. There ain't no better than to bleed at love's demand and let the wounds beg of my dumb.

Peering at, peering down, his mouth agog in hate. It is his must, since his gone is far worse pain than any bruises, since he keeps on for to fade, the light come up and burning like fire becomes of paper, and him yet hovering there and eyeless face, fading despite my pleading.

Birds take to a song; she knows you hate the noise. Afeard to break your look, afeard to anger, she says she's to hold the faith, for she'll be faithful to his rebuke and the beats of your goodbye shall abide with her the day, to welcome you again and better, if but given another blow.

He takes her vow.

Fading, less in body than a spider's web at noon, his mouth is chirps and jitters in the last of the night's crickets, so sad as farewells must, and stealing the final breath, busts itself in air. Then stays a blankness true.

Fearful if I move I hint the scorn for what's been doled to me this day, I stay right fixed on where you shown, to clench my gaze on all the while, since she must work to do your bid.

Inside there bids a bed. The rousing of her guard, and she is called back abed, to scatter the air, catching mayflies in her palm if but to fondle her figure's dregs, since in she goes, legs too wet for bed, and nothing left this day but the long wait for the night.

4

The frantic drumming of hooves flouting the noon of its silence. She looked out and saw Old Totem speeding unto Les and knew that within the code of those drumming hoofbeats there held the summons to whisk him away. Edward kept beside him, Annora out of sight.

"Well, it's finally happened," said Scannell. "Ramsey's gone and anted a thousand volunteers for the state's regiment. He's calling a three-month tour. What you say, old boy? You and Eddie up to enlisting?"

In the gap that followed she heard the horse fight at the bit, birds whose calls were lost in quest of a mate, and she knew he had already made up his mind. His decision an essence, a necessity inherent to the day, which to imagine time without would be to unimagine oneself.

"You don't have to tell me twice, Mister Scannell," said the boy. "I'd love to shoot me some rebs as fast as I can pull—"

"Hush," Les told him.

Even the air seemed to bow, repentant.

Just then the twins came up, bearing a pale. Les sent them in. Annora fumbling at her work, putting the twins to work in quiet.

"Well, we counting you in or not?" said Scannell. "There's only a thousand seats, and every two-bit loafer from here to Mankato who'd rather pick off rebs than break his back in farmwork is riding off east at the edge of his pants. So what'll it be, old boy?"

She dared a glance at the window and in the instant saw nothing. The bright violent day seeming to chastise sight itself.

"All right," Les told him.

Scannell hurrahed, and she could feel Edward inwardly rejoicing because he came from the same stuff as Les.

"You hear that noise? That's the sound of rebs just heard they's death knell. Son, this is your lucky break. You ever wanted the chance to kill a man, you can pick off rebs till your heart's content and get off at it scot-free. I'ma go round up Gruhn. Ain't no better shot than—"

"Don't," he said.

Everything about her balled into a fist.

"Gruhn's been laid up sick. Annora's been going there, tending him. I'm sure word will get around. Gruhn, I know, ought to learn."

Then he was gone.

She waited there, fiddling with her hands, trying to make it seem that she had not heard what she had, but she was sure all of her betrayed herself. She tried to address the twins, but before she parted her lips she heard bursting from her throat the contours of Les's voice, demanding the reason why she had listened, so against her face she hid her hands. Fending off the clamor of Old Totem as he raced down the hill, the uniform resolution of his hooves picking up speed, his rhythm the sound of news, dying, eventually dying, charging the distant ranks of oblivion whereunto he himself dissolved.

When the footsteps entered it was too late. She could no longer try to do or wait. Caught as she was, she could only hope this terror would be the pitying sort.

She stood there, face against her hands, listening, ready, unmoving. If only she kept still, perhaps he would go away. After a while she heard his tread, which bore the voice of her eldest son.

"Mother," he said, afraid that touching would make it worse. "I guess you heard. Mister Scannell said they need volunteers. It'll only be three months, and we'll be back when you need us most. I guess this is farewell."

Under his weight no board shifted, and she imagined him swooping off in the guise of a dustdevil or storm, taking down thousands as he stretched out his wings and turning about and returning all within the span of seconds so that it could mean what it was supposed to and be done so the lot of them could move on.

Then the wood told her he'd gone, a whimpering conversation as the tread withdrew. She listened as he bid farewell to the twins, as he tried to allay their questions, listening yet when the fear began to lurk again and creep as to freeze her skin and beat her heart until it outright stopped—simply one long, immense, thunderous beating—herself nothing but the husk in which the order became fulfilled, listening with him through the silence.

She heard his legs stride up and settle him inches behind. Powerless not to want to become the voice.

Between their flesh she felt the heat that construed the passage of his order, and in it she heard him telling: "You know there are things for men and which men alone can do, the greatest of deeds in history being endeavored without the company of women. I have shown you the justice locked inside every task and have hammered home the best routine for gain, and I am trusting in your competence to think as I do and anticipate my words, objections, and to nip them before my rage can vomit forth while knowing full well you will not come close to meeting the good of my will. Because there is only trusting your ineptitude. But should I have faith in even that, I am more than aware you would find some new channel for oozing your inability. Therefore I leave you the greatest of presents any wife can be left by her husband: hatred of my return and wishing me far away where you will never hear the sting of my tongue or feel the bite of my hand, thus granting you freedom to do and say what you wish."

His legs clipped him out as if they were coursing with that same resolution she had heard in Old Totem's hooves.

Then they two were gone.

If she had been stronger, she would have cried.

Weeks past, meaningless as time. An eternity would not have been so painful, rather have mitigated it, since at least in eternity you resign yourself to the ceaseless torments instead of awaiting a release.

At nights she forbore the bed, preferring to fall asleep in the chair where she could stay ready lest someone enter, positioned to greet them and welcome them, to sally the list of chores she had worked to venture, the appropriate habits as one would stammer out a doubtful roll-call. Further, she felt that if she entered the bed it signaled an invitation, that the voices beyond the barrier would immediately catch wind of her breach and come crashing through the walls and windows, all clambering to mount the bed.

News traveled that Lincoln had extended the three months into three years. Disbelief carried off the town—every lady wore her red-eyed badge—for usually when a number oversoon exceeds its measure it brings an ease, a joyful bounty, which would have followed in celebration, but which now produced a greater reason to fear.

There was word just as she learned the men had marched through the capital and had boarded a train that would whisk them away to Lincoln who would view them and approve them that the Sioux had learned of the men's absence and had banded with teams of thieves, locals whose intimate knowledge bespoke which homes had been left and which of them had stayed and where the valuables lay for plunder.

In town she saw faces contorted as with a certain hunger. She felt a wobbly lamb, one that can barely see and ignorant it is about to be picked up and devoured.

At night she kept the gun between her knees. Although she had never been shown how to use it or been told whether it was hers to touch, she perceived its sense of harm, that she could point and threaten into mistaking that she may, its latent potency the same as its terrible might.

Then one night she heard them breathe.

She had fallen asleep in the chair, the gun raised in her lap, when there came a panting beyond the window. A secrecy of footsteps, whispers. In the center of the cabin Les had built a trapdoor and dug a small pit, which served its use for a root cellar, but she was sure she bore the memory of him exacting again and again that this must be their safety during a time of danger, that this was where they must be. Yet her legs stayed effectively frozen: she knew that if she moved and opened the door and called the twins they would hear and enter long before their escape. Tensed, she listened, quivering from her seat.

Soon the voices sank to the sound of her own breathing, and she woke up, starting, wondering whether she had dreamed and merely caught herself, having slipped in a second's sleep.

There came news of a battle, disastrous for the men. Then a second. What hope they had saved, that the Union would lick them before the three months ran, that they would garner a quick victory, was squandered before spent, and there was emptiness and waiting.

Before then she had never considered getting a letter (she thought that Les and Edward would return whenever they could trust the task for which they were summoned would no longer bother but stay fixed); yet now, certain she would get no letter, her image of them fighting and triumphing and instilling victory into the South began to quake and thin, and while she continued to see them together going about the war, almost savoring the proud fact so that it became a sort of memory she was able to take comfort in, something of the image was beginning to fade, as that scene of them began to be infiltrated by a slight grain of resentment.

No letter came, but her idea of them as she had known them forsook her day by day, and after a while she came to hold the frayedmost feeling that they were out there somewhere—doing what—not even fighting, she could not say.

Still keeping watch, upright in her chair, the periods she slept she slept dreaming in the same position. Tremendous gasps startled her awake. She had managed to bring in the crop and retain the look of things, with all but a few stolen chickens.

She was awake one night when again she heard the breathing. It came as one: a forceful man's deep breath. Calm because it felt so certain about what it hoped to achieve. Yet under the intent she knew there were others of them hiding or they had trained themselves to breathe together.

The gun stood in her lap, where it perched every night, but now she grasped its futility. The windows creaked, pressed from without. She could see them there, lending substance to the dark.

Less sprung from flight than determination to meet the occasion in a way she could account for, she sped the length of the room and sought the twins, picking them up out of sleep, their tired faces opening like buds. She hushed them before they could stir, and flinging the trapdoor out, she ushered them down.

Then they were waiting in dark beyond night. One of them lay at her foot and was crying. Overhead, tensed with listening, she heard footsteps transgress the planks. A leisurely curiosity. Such pacing as marauders who know they will not get caught.

No one had spoken a word.

Then in the close space of the den the footsteps lingered, stopped.

It was the strangest quiet: as if they had come for the purpose of enacting a tableau, each one of them in his pose, an arrangement that required a stranger's dwelling and demanded the unique moonbeams that meandered through her window, each one of them drifting to his place to perform the arrangement of Unstoppable Encroachment.

She strained, hoping to listen. Perhaps she had fallen asleep and they had gone, but at her straining the ladder rung popped and on the instant the trapdoor swept open, was flown from overhead, and she was borne off the rung of the ladder, thrown upon the bed.

The darks of them grouped in pools were hunched in their intent. For why they had stolen in, there seemed no reason but one. She screamed out, hoping someone would hear but knowing no one would. A hand shot forward and struck her; she cowered on the bed.

Then a remarkable man of outstanding figure, apparent from the others, his clothed in new garments that smelled of fresh-tanned leather and expensive dye, stood over her, swelling with reason. What she beheld made her whole person go numb. What thoughts she had of defense, of fighting or appealing to kindness, fear completely felled, as though this incubus had feasted on her will. She shied from scratching or biting for fear this would cause him pain.

He left, then another.

When they were done she expected to be shot. Instead they left her like a thing beyond hope of mending and went not looking back.

Shivering in the dark, tears crested her eyes, her body a great gaping wound. She could feel her heart knocking, trying to escape. So this was the sense that all men felt when dying on the field. The same sensation that Les and Edward had performed long ago in some place far away, and they had sent these messengers as a manner to reclaim her.

And thereupon she was visited by a radical thought: What if the men had shot her indeed? What if they had fired a shot directly into her brain and she was dead? What if they had killed her, but killed her before she was instructed, and she no time to prepare she was moving to the spirit world? What if everything around her, herself included, was dead, no longer existed, because it had merged so well with death?

After a time spent listening and wondering how she could still breathe despite being dead, she saw dawn begin to encroach as it always had, the frail, pale light of which filled the weird serenity with another custom from the world she had left behind. Her gown stuck to her in an unbecoming fashion of someone she was not. She smoothed it back. It hurt to stand. Peering over the rim, she saw the twins fast asleep at the bottom of the cellar, locked together like swimmers on the floor of the ocean.

She went to the window and checked the plains: they lay eddying in the morning clouds. All looked as it had, and yet something somehow had changed, had let go part of itself that had long been firmly entrenched and that part's death had become amputated from the living. Yonder it seemed—the hills, the plains, the clouds, her fingers—a world as near as fiction, a view somehow estranged and farther from the one she was used to seeing, strange but strangely familiar, as if she were watching as someone else, so that even though there was a foreignness, an anonymous distance, nothing in fact had changed.

Each night they returned, and each night she was ready. Only she was sure to hide the twins while she confronted them herself, for they would not presume to think that with one so bold others should be hiding.

There were groups of them, different bands. Sometimes she thought she saw the same men joined up among new partners, their features delineated against the shadows; sometimes they were wholly unknown to her, come perhaps because word had spread or because they knew if they didn't others would.

She thought they might be Indians, deserters, eluders of conscription, or maybe a stew of criminals, ruffians drawn up from the territory who had fallen off the brink and relished a life among the boneyards where they were free to seek their whims rather than abiding near the edge. She thought she saw Union and Confederate uniforms, war paint, half-monstered men in animal pelts, pomade shining off the moneyed curious come to speculate from the East, smelled the distinctive musk of those who had subsisted on the land for generations, the ambergris of the leisured. They were all overpowering, strong in different ways. But she knew she had to protect them, that if ever they should find the children sleeping a few feet below it was over. So she continued to meet them, doing her best to stifle the screams until they were gone and done.

Then it really was over.

One night—by then most of the men who had lived had come home and got their farms revived but not before they had been celebrated at a banquet at which the regiment's spent flag served as a sort of table decoration, the tears and bulletholes rendering it more a violated carcass than a glorious symbol, while select heroes of them had turned around and immediately reenlisted and were thrust right back into carnage, their insistence on bravery having struck her as something natural to her husband—in they trespassed, only on this occasion they were followed.

As she was wont, she fended them off. Shrieking and howling, though not enough to be hurt. Her great fright choking her to paralysis as the great hoard urged upon her, but unlike those times here they suddenly stopped.

Still leaning over her. All quiet. As if a magic spell had halted them. Then she heard her brother. It came as a stab to the unwitting air:

"No."

And just as quickly gunfire crowded the house.

Men collapsed on the bed. She felt them stiffening, their dark visages stitched with terror, appalled at this recognition of Death. Shouts rang from outside, and then a flame sprang through the window to signal Hell itself had attacked.

With the intrusion of smoke men were gasping or dying. In the harrowing brilliance she watched the bodies amass. Pain vivified their expressions, stamping their faces a seal for the underworld. She heard running and then horses speed past the side and then shots fired at the sky.

By now the entire inside shone noonbright and there were bodies smoldering and clogging the air with thick screens of pungent smoke; the few that lived—flames were devouring their legs and arms—capered as they went. She watched one tease from his holster a scalding pistol and scarcely hold it in time to level at his brains and pull the trigger.

"There!"

Gruhn kicked open the trapdoor. A cloud effloresced into which he descended. In a moment a withy child lapped up from the depths. Then another heft up.

Under each arm he took a twin, his good leg leading, and evoked her from the house.

The walls and roof roared like the throat of an angry god. Amid the jeers of logs snapping and plummeting to the floor she scurried across the room but not before catching eyes with a boy lost in the perdition of fire, clutching himself in the corner, his hair curling with flames, and believing this was her son.

"Come," said Gruhn. He took them hence. They found the plunderers had stolen his horse.

Soon the twins were fast asleep in his grip despite their being wrenched at every step. Behind them on the crest and hovering with the steadfastness of the sun, the house that they had built as one would contrive a means of escape. From Gruhn's cabin they could smell the fire.

The next day he returned, bearing news that the house had burnt to the ground, that gone were the livestock, the cattlepen scattered along with the cows, the sheepfold torn along with the sheep, that more of them must have come back in the night, for the fields in their fullness had been razed, so much equipment stolen or wrecked. A state of horrendous ruin.

He told them they had no choice but to stay with him. A few chickens, an ancient goat he had used for milk, and a bald vegetable patch were all that was there. He said he would put her to work and she would have to do as he said.

He made her reclaim the fields, rebuild the pens, gather the smashed limbs of fencing either to salvage or use for kindling; there were orchards to save from grief. Her back became stooped, her hands and feet slow and wavering. By herself she got it near to working again. What they did not eat Gruhn brought to town to sell.

Often he was gone for many days hunting or on surveying trips or scouting the movements of Indians and now and then leading parties against the Dakota, often bringing with him a twin, interchanging one for the other, both of whom he had taught to become fair marksmen, but always there was one who stayed and whose job it was to remain on guard lest the thieves ever come back.

He demanded she share his bed. The twins slept on the floor, later in buckskin cots. When at first she slunk and resisted, he struck her and said from now on she was his to manage and must not question him.

What at first felt wrong and uncomfortable quickly formed the pattern of days. They were living as man and wife. No one told them different, and the few they saw seemed to exude relief, as if two loose cannons had been fettered together and chunked overboard, far from harm's reach. Entreating them, a pleading in her gaze, until no one visited them any longer.

All there was for her was work. Her hair had become quite blanched and her face thin and hollow and her body smaller if tough like leather.

She worked day after day, and she worked ceaselessly and without thought. To her impotent disinterest, a profound fatigue seemed to have besieged her while serving to buttress her absolute collapse, so that the mental inch demanded in remembering a thing from even a moment ago or in planning some next step was now rendered that inch too far and continued to lie beyond her advent. Whatever stamina she relied on to work had intruded against her brain and tapped its strength, leaving her in a pitifully constricted present the way a horse must view his task when equipped with the aid of blinders, except hers of the two was the more restricted.

As the fields came up and went back, as she tended the babies of the grandchildren of animals she did not remember, it was fitting she should arise one day and find a space where the twins should sleep. No sign telling where or why they had gone, it may as well have been they never existed. If she had been asked right then what their names were they would have proved impossible for her to recall.

Gruhn looked on in dwining silence. Rare was the instant and shocking when he of necessity spoke. It shattered the room like dynamite, and in the blind debris she crawled, picking up pieces that had composed her thoughts, the task of claiming them amid the rubbage having lunged her beyond response.

To hear her footsteps plodding after her, to feel the stare of her shadow, its grinning back, struck her with mortal terror. There was nothing that, from a gaze, would not wield insidious hate. Only at nights, once the shadows had disappeared and her feet desisted from tagging her, that world of fears abated. She lay there tensed with dread at the sudden enlivening of his snore.

Before he came he had long revealed himself. The night had been primed with readying, its noiseless capacity tested to host this guest, worries dismissed as you would shake the dust from the blankets, so that when he did it felt entirely right.

As soon as she saw him she knew what he required. Slipping from bed then through the door, she held the certainty of a raindrop. Her mission she sensed to the quick, duty the same as instinct. Yet on reaching out, in welcoming him to her arms, the audacity of a smile daring from her lips, just as she allowed herself to yearn toward him, draw near, she was startled to grasp his retreat. As she advanced, he departed. Then when she paused, she was startled to find he had stopped. Hovering there, drifting, his great blankness a featured absence of sorts, a hubris that shunned mistakes. And within that absence a strength that urged, incited her to seek that which was beckoning mere paces yonder—but when she moved, then he—and they continued like that ever yonder until he led her back just as dawn was creeping east. Then, still rich in pursuit and determined to welcome him still, to cling him to her being, she watched him fade. Then gone.

Though his presence continued to stay as she moved through the day, sensing him though not seeing, borne upon the currents of Gruhn's demands as if drifting in eternity where everything had gone extinct and swayed among lost shadows of itself like willows in a gale, nothing to pretend but trim them back, until at night once again, the body beside her in a rage of quiet, fields of silhouette, the window firm with waiting, into her sight he would come hanging in the moonglow, keen for her tempting as any hummingbird for his nectar, and she as keen to follow.

5

With a loudness constrained they were rapping his door while checking the neighboring houses lest they rouse anyone by mistake. Their heart kicking in their gullet, for these were the opportunities they most risked being caught.

The door dropped open and out of it slung a barrel in their face as if something for them to taste. The old man was winking to make sense of the dark or did not believe what stood before him.

"Thieves!" he stammered, but already he was scanning the horses wrangled in the yard.

"Shhh!" said Quinn, showing him his hands, that he held nothing.

"We ain't here to rob you, old man. We got something you might care to praise."

"Oh yes thieves you boys are."

Hesitant, he stepped out from his den, forth from the cavernous dark. Wrenching his neck and checking if there was anyone sighting him at the end of the street, from behind a porch, up on the gables. He gave the impression of a half-wrung rooster.

"You boys may not be robbing me directly," he said, "but someone's had to pay, and I suspect you may've done chipped in." He spoke this, noting Quinn's swollen socket.

"And here I thought we was friends," said Irving.

"Friends, bah!" the old man huffed. "We ain't friends. Ain't never been friends. You're somewhere between a

31

stranger and a acquaintance. I hope these dobbins ain't branded."

"You gonna look at them or not?" said Quinn.

In the bluish remnant of night he went around, smacking his lips and muttersome, at once skeptical and wholly decisive, within the words themselves two sides that seemed to contest and vie (had he not just spoken to them they would have thought he was crazy). Pulling up hooves and squinnying into mouths and flicking his nails against teeth and running his palms along gaskins and counting the pace of heartbeats and turning up tails and peering in with the cunning of a jeweler inspecting a diamond of long-winded renown, taking especial pains over a thumb-width whorl of scar, studying a blaze as if he were preparing to declaim his thoughts on some renowned work of art he had always heard championed but himself had never chanced to scrutinize until this moment, he gave the impression of omniscient perspicacity, of reading their entire lives and every singularity from the planting of gestation to their standing before his home.

"Well, what you think?"

At that the old man snapped from his great reckoning—so suddenly he appeared to have lost all interest, some stake in him uprooted like a tent swept away in a gust—whereupon he sighted his powerful attention against the twins, who were watching him intent.

"Well?"

"I can do fifty," said Hancock. His figure looked cold and dead out there in the cold, dead morning.

"You can do fifty what?"

"He can't do fifty nothing," Quinn said.

"I'll give you fifty dollars, and that's the end of my crossing point."

It came as shocking when repeated.

"For which horse?" Quinn asked. He said it not quite as a whisper.

"It ain't for which," said Hancock. "The fifty stands for all."

"For all?" yelled Irving, running his grip along his belt. "Why hell, what about the Thoroughbred? He alone is worth at least a hundred. At least a hundred."

Hancock spat; his stare was as fixed as marble.

"Boys, that horse has the worst case of thrush on her hind legs I ever seen in forty years of being open for business and is past curing to sin. See that leaning atoe? Why you'd be better off just shooting her than sinking your time and money in thrush, but she ain't hardly worth the price of your bullet. In fact, I wouldn't take her if you paid me to. Come to think of it—and I ain't just being nice but to show you boys how serious I do despise a thrush—you boys go on and keep that one who ain't worth the hour of higgling and I'll give you the fifty for the rest of them. You can split that real even down the center like."

"Shoot," said Quinn, "we can take them to somebody else. Somebody not bent on swindling their best customers. Donoghue's always fair."

"Ha! I'm sure they'll be doubly wanted at Donoghue's!"

"Damn," said Irving. He was picking at his belt. "What's so wrong with the rest of them? I've watched them run a week, and I'll be damned if they're all bad. I'd be proud to sit my ass on any them steeds."

At that the old man burst out a laugh, short but stern and bumptious.

"What's so bad?" It was a scoff the way you'd tell a blind man that the reason it was so loud and reeked of smoke was because you were trundling him through the same battlefield that had just gone and blinded him. "Why I'd say whoever it was who you boys robbed, I'd say they was the cheapest sons of bitches ever to run ahorse. That or didn't know nothing about choosing jades. That or lost a hand of cards one right after the other and traded their last pair of pants for these here sorry plugs I'd hate to lump with the proper name of horses."

"Well, what's so wrong with that Paint?" he asked him, almost a dare.

"Boy, both them Paints got bull necks no serious rider's ever gonna look at twice, not when he can buy a better-shaped neck for a fair price. Those Arabian's pasterns are too upright, and she's already got arthritis, as I'd be happy to point out, and that's just gonna get worse. This Morgan's barrel is gonna pop like a dead dog in the sun bout any day cause he's got abdomen troubles. And, fellas, that Appaloosa must be staler than my grandmother's milk. You pay my sincere respects when he kills over on you and you're singing 'Fare Ye Well' out at the trailhead."

"Let's just take them to Donoghue's," said Irving, wanting to rid himself of the trader whom he would rather agree with than continue hearing. "Donoghue's bound to pay at least a hundred. I don't know why we keep on coming back to this guy."

"Shoot," said Quinn. "He'll be dead before he takes his next squat."

"Okay," said the man. He became erect and rigid. "I'll give you a hundred for the lot of them. But that's only so you don't go waking up poor Donoghue and wasting the time of a friend."

Some while before sunup they left the town, the constant hooves firing strong and rampant since they had freed themselves of the caravan, which had parted from them like the guilt of a bad deed, the fresh thunder almost blameless. They agreed on going north because the trail was not much traveled, after a few days to veer northwest until they alighted on or near Utica.

The sun crept over the horizon, illuminating the gray plains of clouds choked overhead, but you would scarcely have known it, for, rendering a light almost without shadow, it remained behind them, black rolled-out clouds almost purple at their centers, like an actor forbidden to come on stage. The manic galloping and wind boiling to an insane drumbeat, they heard only the thick, magnificent pounding, the quoping of heart or hooves or of the beating that had crept through their legs, inspiring their veins into beating in wild unity, the wind cresting like rushes from an undiscovered waterfall. A flock of geese shot past, evasive of being caught. The rich feast of speed spilled out vociferous of all words, the terrific pleasure, the ludic gestures, the part-attempts to stand in the stirrups and extend their view to that of a titan striding the air and with that the solace that even if the old man had swindled them yet ahead lay a wealth so immense and wonderful their best winning streak would seem a downright cheat to compare. Glancing back now and then to ensure no one was following them.

When he woke he had the whole sky in his face and the vicious doubloon of noon as paled through clouds. It did not take long to verify that a lone rider was coming, his pace a drifting walk.

As he approached they saw he was missing a right arm, and almost upon them that he was riding without a salient weapon. He had almost passed when one of them called, "Hold it."

He curbed his mule. He clicked until the mule fulfilled the turn. The stranger, seeming rather shocked, met the leveled guns.

"You're awful trusting to go about unarmed," said Irving.

The stranger grimaced and studied their copied faces: neither twin was smiling.

"Maybe I am," he offered. "Or maybe it's hiding and I'm awfully quick on the draw."

"You'd have to be awful fast," said Quinn. "And that hid gun a whole lot nearer than your mule's ass. How about getting off the saddle, boy."

Soon they were grouped together while one of them emptied out the sad contents of his sack and the other one rifled his pockets. Despite his obvious want he stood there lank and jaunty, too blithe for these dark circumstances.

"What's so damn funny? I'm gonna blow that grin off your idiot cheeks."

"It's just that . . ." He was holding up an arm and a half. "It's just that I do believe I recognize you fellas. Say, you're Quinn and Irving Tamplin, ain't you boys?"

In tandem they cocked their pistols.

"Now what'd you have to be so smart for? Now you know we can't let to leave you alive. Even if you do solemnly swear you ain't gonna spill the beans you'll only be swearing a lie. But you can't even put your hand on a book and do that, can you now, Mister Armstrong?"

"You'll be sure to fix us to the first some bitch who takes you in," said Irving. "Even if you do only have a worthless mule and two lousy dollars and nineteen cents."

"But you really don't know who I am?" said the stranger.

Slowly he raised his hand and tipped back his hat and grinned down on them as if the grinning were supposed to explain. For him to say that—ever since they had first perceived him there had been something about him almost deliberately held back and containing a singular purpose, held back from revealing itself since glimpsing his kind of face. The twins, who were still aiming their guns but had forgotten about sticking up the familiar stranger that maybe they had run with at some point beyond their ken, stared and were waiting for it, until, drawing them on, reproachful, the thing struck them with the joy of a childish punishment and at once jogged them to the past.

"No!"

"Why hot damn! Brother?"

"Yep."

"No!"

"Yes!"

"Brother?"

"I know! Crazy, isn't it, boys."

They rushed in. Confusion around a handshake, they ended in a competition of hugs, a greeting muddled in excitement. At last there were sober left-handed handshakes.

"I can't believe it."

"What in the hell are you doing out here and all alone without no gun?"

"We figured you was dead."

"I know, I almost figured the same myself."

"Gosh," frowned Irving, "sorry about holding you up. We weren't planning on going to kill you. We just didn't know it was you."

"Really," he said, "it's okay."

"No, it ain't, brother," said Quinn. "Now you tell us what the hell you're doing out here and all alone before we do you in for real."

They chuckled and went silent.

"That's just it. I was on my way to Shoal Creek to see if I'd find you boys. I'd have written you a letter, but I didn't plan too far in advance. I didn't have money and figured I could use the trip." He paused to let that shunt a while. "So," he fumbled, "who all's home these days?"

They continued looking at him, this man made from disbelief. Still waiting for him to vanish, to admit his hallucination, feeling he might imminently disappear the second they blinked or uttered breath. Both leaning on the other, the elder nodding, encouraging.

"We ain't been back in maybe about nine years," said Irving. "It might could be bout nine."

"Yeah, staying away makes sense."

"Last we saw, we was all living with Uncle Gruhn."

"What? And Mother too? And Mother?" He said this instantly. "But with Father there, though, right?"

"No, just her. We thought he was with you."

In spite of the evenness he had shown a moment ago, he had become unhinged, his face springing dark crimson and his hand fumbling at, massaging the nub. The twins still so spellbound they could have remained on their heels until dusk.

Then, unnoticed as a shift in wind, part of him seemed to turn, collect itself, which he completed by letting go a long and doleful sigh, and retrieving a soiled bandana, catching his hat in the pit of his arm, he mopped his brow.

"I guess I should have come home sooner. Is that where you're headed now? You were going to Shoal Creek, but then I nearly let you murder me?"

Now it was the twins' turn to fumble. Both of them kicked the ground; they stabbed it and drew small Xs with the toe of their boot. Edward watched them speculate how to best cover their business until one deferred to the other and that one raised up at him and said:

"We's running north a spell. Got work moving this chap and drove. He asked us to scout and be his guide. He hired us for protection."

The elder nodded, a nod that showed he could be counted on if needed to lie.

"I see. Well, I don't want to keep you and go getting in the midst of your business."

"No!" they said at once.

He looked at them, ostensibly confused.

"You ride with us, Ed, you want," said Irving. "We ain't going to Shoal Creek, but we'll be getting within a day's ride. When we get off to our split, you just cut off from us then. I mean, how's that work with you?"

"I'd say that works just fine."

Sort of nodding and almost whistling, he returned to put back his chattels. He kicked them to a heap, dirt and everything, sort of nodding and faintly whistling, an amused lightness to his manner as if he found himself once again executing a bad habit he had not altogether given up hope of ridding. Not quite adroit to lift his provision sack on the first attempt. Swinging the sack on his mule and tying the strings hand and teeth. They watched him cast himself up and reach for the reins, his iron-stern smiling. Something about his air evocative of a man who has just finished digging himself out a grave. He squinted at them, grinning.

"So long as I'm your first stick-up, and I ain't gonna get busted from associating with two known felons. I couldn't get used to the idea of being a wanted man."

They were biting their tongue, but in mounting their horses they finally burst out laughing. Edward joined them, and they started to move.

Quinn was the first to talk.

"Don't you know you got to lean into the law otherwise you get knocked down?" He said this almost a shout, his voice swallowed among the cold shoulders of hills. "How come you ain't for riding with no gun?"

Already the horses were well ahead of him, his inert mule strained to its limit.

"I've fired enough guns. And I'm faring fine without one. I survived my run-in with you okay."

"That's cause we let you live," called back Irving.

On his mule, to their backs, Edward made an aristocratic bow, an obeisance that seemed to say, That is true— or rather, That is only true because I allowed it.

Before him the fields lay in their frozen undulations while against them the grass billowed and sped like one sea on another. By the edge of the trail gangs of sparrows were preening themselves in the dirt, which the clabbering hooves troubled, dividing brothers and sisters perhaps never to meet again. Across the sky the clouds had woven a great gray blanket. An extensive flock of geese sailed past as though pointing the direction he should take.

"Mind if I inquire," yelled Edward, allowing a breath to pass before he pursued the thought, "what happened to your eye? It doesn't look so . . . sightly."

They continued walking, his brother pretending he had not heard. He hoped he would not probe him in return about the arm.

Then, quick as a change in wind, he turned back toward him, contentedly pleased.

"It looked at something it weren't supposed to see!"

6

When they reached Holger's they found a myopic old veteran seated at a table around which appeared to generate a vortex of men intending to enlist. A few heads turned and watched them come up. What they saw were two faces of one person: the older and its copied revision, father and son having lived together so long in that cramped cabin, they had ended up mirroring each other in a way that went beyond ordinary family resemblance, since everything about the son—his carriage, his gestures, his intonation (and which led you to assume his thoughts)—had become a lesser replica of the prototype. Not that he ever did, but had he met his father's acquaintances they would have dealt him the same respect they offered when seeking the man.

Les gave him the reins and told him to wait. Edward watched him part through the mass that folded back for a second before closing on themselves. Soon he was obscured amid the frenzy.

With his thumbnail he picked at the chaffing leather and studied a beetle navigating the braids. The sun dampened and rekindled, the earth seeming to pulse until all was shadow.

After a while he saw him fight back through the crowd. Above all the heads he was holding a certificate and a ten-dollar note.

"Did they give you that, father?" said the boy. "I thought they were only taking volunteers. They must have really wanted—"

"I want you to rent a room." To his forehead he held the note, the son recoiling, perhaps sensing it was some kind of weapon. "You go to Perez's boarding house, and you stay there two nights. You tell him I sent you. After that you can enlist."

The boy still blenching, the man forced the paper into his hand. Edward, staring at him still, not trying to figure the reason for his change of mind but perceiving that if there were a purpose it lay at such a depth that rendered reckoning impossible.

"Take it! Are you blind?"

He looked down and beheld the sterile beauty of the dollar's art, which propounded somewhere in the colors, lines, and texture was the mystery of his plan.

"Yes, sir," he said, and took back his hand.

Les watched him. His manner that of a spring wound to constriction, but seeing in him that agreement to do his will, that the dollar had justly served as distraction to cover the farewell, he squeezed the boy once on the shoulder, getting the feeling he was hovering, and then marched off.

They assigned him to B Company and made him a first lieutenant. The air celebratory, buzzing, saccharine, the odor that which good and simple baking can emit, where you become a little dizzy with the breathed-in sugar you know you will soon ingest, sweeping them along the festive days and nights. Sleep mocked by pleasurable howls. Gunsmoke flowered at the moon and other impossible targets.

Some of them had never traveled this far east, most not since they were children. Something inherent to the excitement, the collective eagerness to fight, that in returning to the roots from before they had severed and ventured forth they would return to a dead stump that would lend itself to easy defeat, and given the added vitality through which the severing had availed them.

Before they had begun serious training Lincoln extended their three-months-term into three years. A few voices worried the fun. At worst it seemed to multiply the holiday idleness to indefinite luxury; no one wanted to go back even if there was concern about who and what they had left.

It was as though the war had breached an incredible hiatus in their lives, as though the silent men of forgotten youth who had labored demure to fate had all these years been suffering under the pretense of a happiness that thinly disguised real agony while ignoring the best of their dreams when suddenly a chasm had cleft the ground, and now that they had been granted the task of scaling it there lingered scarce question of whether they would achieve that which they set out to win, the primary encumbrance being how to outmaneuver the thousands of other adventurers that were vying for the same renown. Understood it was though inarticulate, they knew they were also to fight each other.

After three months of training and enough marching to imprint the mud with the fossil of their boredom for ages to come, just when the original tour should have expired as had the final turns from idleness into drudgery, they saw battle—the training and drills and marching up like the whorl of a cannonball.

Men shouted orders that were torn to howls as companions charged or fled. Strewn limbs led into bodies that were attached to them no longer and hails of bullets stung the air like furious insects to finish themselves on their recipients. A dense cloud drifted in, settling a falsenight over the field so that many were forced to shoot on hearing alone or found themselves bayoneted, their killer rushed out of the fog, their joining ended as soon as met.

Night set as an essence that had already been long present, and the strangers it revealed were the carcasses of friends intertwined with Death, their egregious contortions, these final postures, attitudes so personal, so private. Only the drunk slept that night. Loud was the air and leaden with lowing men; those who listened listened with divine despair.

A week later they fought again. Those who had rejoiced that they had survived the last battle now cursed themselves for staying alive. Their feet exulting them over corpses, launching them over cannons, sporadic fires, leaping between bullets, any devious route to breath. Fallen comrades who should have been dead looked up and shouted encouragement then died. Again a pseudonight palled the miserable activity, causing friend to fire on friend or soldier against captain and the struck to retaliate. The ground in constant paroxysm sending up like April shoots generations of worms twitching and quickening. Many were trampled; those who weren't were often shot while attempting to extricate themselves from traps of viscera.

As the fighting began to quell, a chorus rose from the field. That was a music heard by the damned. Throughout the night the living yelled for the dying to hurry and kill themselves, though they continued all through the night as ceaseless as the sea. Occasional shots still firing from perhaps a handful of brute fellows who had not been told the battle had broken.

It went on like that for a week. Smoke and clouds became permanent, skin and uniforms swart shadows that vaulted, cavorted, danced, enacting a bizarre new form of minstrelsy. Each night before he went to bed, Colonel Colvill reported the tally of losses to the regiment; then one night, waiting for him to appear, they watched him lurk past like a beaten animal, neither a glance nor greeting, and go fix himself in his tent.

As a semblance of summer wore on they marched back north. Wading through rivers and dismal rains, waters that soiled their garments and made their uniforms permanent things of stains, water drunk hot from boiling.

Every new roll call exposed a heightening absence of deserters who had slipped off into the marsh. Those who stayed began to age at a scandalous rate: boys began to look like fathers, fathers like septuagenarians; everyone grew stooped and bent and cynical.

By fall the regiment had lost enough weight to equal a third of its original mass. Ghastly and unbecoming, they formed a ragged army, suggesting someone had exhumed them from a better war in history, knowing the dead will continue to fight.

It was September, the battle over a three-mile stretch of land. There had been several pretty houses and barns, elegant predecessors of the estates they had built back home, but these were now pocked and mutilated by errant shot and looked the very brothels of target practice. Fields that had once waved their store bursts of canister and the volleys of rifles had leveled save here and there a pathetic stalk and some shrub assaulted of her verdure.

Over such ruin Les was forging ahead (he had been made a captain) and was knocked out cold by shrapnel. His men charged on, thinking him dead or as good if they gathered him back to camp.

When he woke there were stars in his eyes and he felt engulfed by motion and smoke and he was conscious of the sensation of a continuous hurtling forward. He lay there caked in mud and without movement among a tableau of carnage.

For a second, he wondered if he was dead. For the life of him he could not get his sight to stay: all was pitching, a drunken nightmare. He felt his head and was puzzled to find no blood. Slowly, overwhelmed by nausea, he got to his feet, the whole earth rearing and pitching him from the mud, and began to walk in the direction he assumed was camp.

Maundering in aimless zigzags. Striking against bodies and cannonpits that tripped him. Pausing to vomit and gag.

Corn was smoldering beside burnt meat. A splintered fence marked the recent traffic of shells. Beyond him in the distance he could hear voices slurred around a fire and he tried aiming himself there.

Then, relieved out of the smoke, he saw a medic whom he nearly failed to signal, a witless pointing at head. Words having abandoned him, not quite absent but yonder the aid of thought and gazing back as if mistrustful and deciding whether they were truly needed or not, he realized too late he was Confederate, both of them widening with recognition before throwing themselves on each another.

A struggle of choking. He had his arms around his neck, but the medic's reach outreached his own. He was struggling to fight him off, fighting to undo his grip. He tried kicking him in the groin. At the second instance the knee came up and thwarted him, though he had to come forward a bit to do this and slackened his grip so he could swallow a morsel of air, his body urging him that his life would forthwith expire.

He pummeled his arms in a last cache of strength. As he felt his entire awareness sink, in a struggle to keep off the blackening onslaught, he lurched and grabbed the pistol, a shadow's thought doubting it was capped and loaded, and spent himself on the trigger. Together they fell.

Yet the hands shot up and found him, their grasp seeking their former impress. He caught his throat in response. Both grips tightening and the insane comprehension that the harder he should squeeze, the harder was clamped his own. Eyes struggling to jettison their sockets. The last he perceived before passing out was a helpless attempt at measuring them, at trying to discern exactly how much life in them had fled and gauging them against what he imagined must be his own. And then everything went like night.

He woke. His breathing was already shallow and he rested on a body. The boy was rigid with quiet, the face a dark flower. He eased his hands from squeezing the medic's neck, then feeling weight around his own, he parted that grip and freed himself and got up and beheld him. The boy lay there at the foot of an old oak, his teeth showing the smallest smile of gratitude, as if his killer had spared him worse pain. A gentle gust came up and blew over his hair.

At his return his men were shocked to see him alive, but in war shock is a platitude, and after retelling his story for barely a day it became just that.

For the rest of the year they followed the Army of the Potomac on a meandering trudge north. Winter came like absence. Les hunched over his porridge, snow trapped in his lashes. He considered his son and he felt no remorse when he found himself wishing he were killed in his initial minute of battle, and if not killed then at least to have had the good sense to flee, and if not fled then at least to go on pretending it meant something more purposeful than it was so that the going on living did not divulge a great stupidity in his breeding.

When spring came with temperate nights and rollicking streams, it hurt to look at the wildflowers, and so they marched watching their feet; their once-beaming faces war had reduced to scowls despite that less than a year of enlistment remained. A few made suicide pacts in their tents.

Once Colvill declined to stop a band that, while they were fording a pretty creek, drifted to the water—on their faces a distracted insouciance not unlike the expression of a mystic answering a supernal call—and sank themselves among the ripples, and for that he was arrested.

A week later they camped where the battle was already underway a few miles distant. The sharp banter of artillery heckling them as they awaited orders.

That night they watched the fire, reading the embers for signs and recognizing, on looking up from the flames, they were seated among ghosts.

Les, on the pretense of keeping an eye out for deserters, found himself slipping into a tent. In it glowed a lamp, which evoked the whispered intimacy of the innermost sanctuary of a temple. What he saw was a soldier sat on his cot and weeping. Les cleared his throat. The lad peered up. Realizing it was Les, he stood to, an embarrassed mess.

"I'm sorry," he said, sniffling. "I just . . . you know . . . they say this one is gonna be awful bad."

He placed a hand on the boy's shoulder, a gesture that felt beyond him, that someone else would have done, for these days he seldom touched his own skin. With that the boy collapsed into tears. Apologizing as you would before a disappointed father. His crying effluent, uncontrolled.

He put another hand on his shoulder, and the boy glanced up, clearly ashamed but grateful, though before he could excuse himself or say anything he had clenched down on his neck, his grip intent, beyond him, as if they possessed a will all their own.

Les watched him sink to the floor. The boy's face began to turn bright purple and his eyes skew on themselves. Their gross derangement seeming to proclaim they could not accept the sight of the coming end. His hideous vulnerability both repelled him and intrigued him. Then his stare sharply spasmed and went out.

Still bent over, he continued to clutch him (perhaps in killing him part of them had consolidated and extrication meant a sort of suicide, or perhaps he was simply afraid that in letting him go he would at once inflate with life). After a time he righted the cot and propped him in his sheets, daring him to inhale, then, convinced the odds were he was dead, he slipped out of the tent and walked, almost a run, while casting behind him now and then to verify nothing had happened.

The next day with Colvill rejoined he listened as his superiors demanded they take a fortified slope. Into the tongue of slaughter. Incredulous that any man should order unblinking the deaths of so many as he would new stiches for his shirtsleeves and not think on it again for the rest of the day.

There were shells shrieking, plagues of bullets swarming for feed. The ground trembled like a horse twitching off flies. As he led them toward the ravine, over a territory where being alive felt somehow wrong, somehow incongruous and guilty, he nearly welcomed the inevitable passage, thinking of those thousands on thousands of unwitting beasts over his life who had spurred no remorse and his holding the just sense that he could go on killing them forever and it would not detract an ounce from his blessedness, that a hundred or hundred million deer or pigs or hens accounted nothing when held up against his soul, and that it was according to this line of reasoning somehow that he and everyone else were able to go on killing each other, since the dead, intrinsically less the instant they were killed, were something like a shot deer that could not be weighed any more, were not even allowed to approach the same scale against the living.

That night he strangled a third. This time he knew he was going to do it before he set about doing it. His target was not in his company or regiment but a runaway African he trailed to his tent.

Returned in the dead of night, he arrived preoccupied and doubted he would be able to work his hands. The thought tormented him like ridding a vexing obsession, a splinter under the fingernail that, until extracted, nothing else is more important, the only thing he could truly be forced to take any interest in regardless of the grandeur of events beyond. He had brought a knife with him just in case, but the fellow never woke, only slipped from one rest to the next. So easy it was and simple he felt he had been summoned, himself the ordained instrument to fulfill some longing, his work a vital necessity.

There, stooped over the dead, he could have almost sworn the corpse was faking, perhaps a ruse to get him to go and, once left, up he would spring, this possum playing dead, his contours and features an impossible heap at the bottom of a lake, his blackness curdled from the dark like obsidian cast on tar. He half-expected to turn and on turning find him hovering there behind, a vengeful figure whose murder must be justified, and he would have continued believing he was not fully dead had he not come back the next morning and walked past the crowd, in the midst of them the carcass.

The fighting grew worse. They ran with soiled pants like a charm or badge of honor. Whirly shells disintegrated, ravened them where they stood. Many turned on themselves in the heat of battle amid their enemies and blew out their brains like the stuff of daffodils.

But from all this he was immune. His recklessness and audacity and what seemed his utter contempt for his own life inspired his men at the maddening pitch to surrender to their destruction and offer their flesh to cannons or as feasts for famished bullets, hurling out ultimate screams, but Les remained unscathed.

Their mess kits rattling with leftover terror, they lined up that night to shake his hand, begged him to get drunk with them, for the secret of his totem or whom he had sold his soul to and where they could trade with such a demon.

The next night there was no fighting, only burials and prayers; they could say they had won the battle. Throughout the camp the wounded writhed, festering like refuse (their amputated limbs burned not far enough away not to upset those who smelled the meat, because one is most sickened by fetors also savory). Since the beginning typhoid had haunted them, though lately it had become a fixture, and the ill, whether they had willed themselves ill or relented from despair, its transient hucksters.

They struck camp; it was announced they were to march to the city and help keep peace because there had been riots. For the first time in months smiles budded on rotten faces. Lips glistening beside fresh wounds. There was talk of celebration and of women, which for the longest spell had been rationed to crumbs.

Nothing had prepared him for the return to urban life. Fighting to stroll down the block. Indifference to the point of antagonism. The entire metropolis staked against yourself.

While his company tiptoed off, leaving him alone to confront the bedlam in his thoughts, he would wander the city in search of someone: not necessarily a soldier or someone who had been to the war, but anybody he saw walking down the street or avenue and that held that sudden burgeoning of congruous selection, a body, he sensed, that possessed the cosmic shibboleth.

He would follow them home and then wait for them to emerge. Often he stayed there, oblivious of the hour, trained on them through the night, until he would follow them the next morning on the route back to work. He came to understand he could go on following them indefinitely, could watch them and never be known, that from behind the constant city he might gaze on them every day and go unrecognized for a stranger, a hitching post, a ghost, invisible; forever watching them, he could become part of the necessary life beyond them that sustained and allowed them to walk the ground. During these drifter's holidays he was grasping with all his might to stay himself.

It was not until he was with a girl one night that he knew he was going to do it. Moonlight draped her splayed breasts, rendering them nacreous and aquatic, a species of invented creature dozing among the reefs of an invented sea. For several hours he watched her heart knock in her throat, and like a hungry wolf he saw himself pouncing on it: her surprised start, his strong arms clutching the life as it kicked and thrashed in an attempt to overcome him, begging to persevere, and his beholding the special look, that tender kernel amid the violence, the appeal to his murderer's pity in reminding him of their common humanity, then expired at its most wildest. She slept there quiet, inviting, her secrecy a kind of gift. But he could not bring himself to do it. He was not reining back so much as no final incitement encouraged him forward. He knew it for the shabby stopgap it was, and he left in the night.

For the first time in a while he thought about Annora. Months had past since she had last flitted through his brain.

During the noon of night, that time not so much a time as dreary span between midnight and daybreak when few of those creatures formed in the feared image of their maker linger yet awake and those that do must be deranged or plotting some treacherous harm, he dwelt on her and what she had done to ruin his farm. He told himself it was possible she had died, been killed, or taken by the Indians he kept hearing about. Then the notion occurred to him—if he had thought about her any earlier it would have come to him then—he was sure that this was what had happened:

Gruhn had taken her. He had seized the gap to reclaim his sister, to turn his sons against him, and would defend them to the utmost. Not only had he been so careless and flagrantly scattered all he had carefully safeguarded and that had required inordinate vigilance, but while he had been a thousand miles aloof and fighting a regular enemy he had let the absolute worst saunter into his home.

Each new second demanded his profound control to stay himself from not racing in that direction. From not grabbing a gun and blowing his brains out to his just punishment. He knew that Gruhn would be, was waiting for him, would sight him long before he ever had hope of sighting him first. Returning would end in death, Gruhn the price of escape.

Then, as if the inner-seething had boiled, melting the nerves, so that a coolness now laved bare bone, he halted, seemed to take a step back, his massive anger having served to wash him clean and rid him of any hope. In this clarity, with the bondage of himself having slipped away, sloughed like a skin under which there was no other skin but a vastness and possibility that knew only immense freedom, he felt alive to the stars and signs overhead and opened in a perspective he had never known before, for an instant becoming a stranger to himself, a perspective that had transfigured his former self into an acquaintance that the years had slowly renounced until what was left had become a shadow of bitter indifference, like the memory of a former lover.

In the ultimate minutes he would allot for them, he resolved never to return to Shoal Creek, that Annora was as good as dead (despite his wishing she were, rather than alive to his careless mistake), that he would never think on any of them again, since clearing the sheets of his memory was the only choice left for the false sacrifice of his home, his land to Gruhn.

Standing alone on the desolate port, the brine of the ocean an aroma he had not considered in twenty-odd years and was shocked to think he had missed, he let go a scream that contained the breadth of all he had just disavowed. He listened to it shrink and echo among the islands. Only the outlandish stars had heard, and they winked they would take this identity among their fires.

They left on a boat called the Empire City. Less than a few months remained to their enlistment, though had it been only a week it would not have made much difference, the dilemma of a solder's life being that the prettiest sunrise may portend the bloodiest dusk.

Back South he returned to his tendency. At first there was no reason to exercise caution: within the randomness of combat these deaths were batted away, an inevitable angel's share. But when it became so random and daily it could not but be deliberate, they issued a warning that someone in the brigade was killing their own.

As a joke soldiers began sleeping with loaded pistols; watches were organized to patrol and interrogate suspicious behavior, as a result of which he forced himself to wait, and for a time he gave up his quest, no resolution ever such torturous cruelty, like a child stumbled into poison ivy and compelled to sit on itchy hands.

News traveled they were to counter Lee's flank along the river, and he felt he must do something. Roaming tents, afraid, but more terrified if he did not. Men eyed him with suspicion, ready for him to divulge himself. He intuited that behind every flap lay a weapon cocked in wait. Still he knew he had to.

Growing momentous, every thought threatening to tear through his breath, the shout of it fomenting within the whisper. He considered throwing himself at their feet and begging to be taken prisoner in order that he might have something to give up for Death, some sacrifice by which he aimed to feed Him and immune himself from ill.

He stayed up the whole night, devising a just plan. In the outset of the charge, while the men were expiring among smoke and screams, he slowed his run until he was a ways behind them and fired on a comrade from the back that he saw was instantly felled. Congratulating himself that no one had witnessed the deed and that he had achieved something too bad, too abominable that even Death was unable to take him that day.

Then it was February and their enlistment came to an end. A date that had lingered forever beyond attainment like a foreign new land that you are told rises beyond the offing, now the hopeful rim sighted along with its myriad possibilities. They were whisked back to the capital where politicians entertained them with receptions. Amid fine wainscoting men were already boasting about reenlisting. He wished neither to reenlist nor return nor did he want to stay and beg to find work in one of the cities. Like an escaped pig turned to boar that is incapable of turning back again, he decided to join the train west, not knowing where it should lead.

The train shuttling them through a dark that blanketed not a terrain so much as a memory disinterred to scarcely the thing it was when buried. They lay sprawled on themselves, empty of dreams, such men that a meager push would trip into the afterworld. He pondered where the urgent need to choke them had gone.

About a hundred miles from his past he worked that spring for an eccentric widower who smoked a calumet whose feathers had become wan barbs, decorations more weaponly than of flight, and who took to sitting down with it at abrupt intervals to chant and prostrate as though he were responding to the song of a muezzin that only he could follow. He heard that Alfred Sulley had been leading an expedition against the Dakota since the winter and he left the farm to join them, his blood quick and hot, desirous.

After a month of hunting he caught up with them and sought the General in his tent. Offering him his papers, a mental tally of the dead he'd made, a number, he wagered, between 242 and 260.

Enter a woman, the General's wife, a handsome Yankton, to pour them tea. Her pinching gold-rimmed china and proper stirring of sugar blasphemous to his sense of her, the perfect etiquette more alien to her than had she come in bouncing on her hands instead of padding on velvet slippers. He fought the impulse to reach for his pistol and blast her from the tent, proclaiming to the mute husband, "There, I have shot you the most dangerous of Sioux."

He was given command of a battery. Soon they caught wind from a wagon train listing for gold that nearby was a whole village, tipis in the thousands. Sully ordered them ahead, their pace ravenous, hungry for a sustenance like food.

A lone Indian who may have been a chief or simply an idiot stepped forth to the ledge of the cliff and signified ribaldry while he barked and shrieked. He seemed swept in the midst of a sublime orgy. Finally they could stand it no longer and down he fell, diving the length of the cliff toward the ravine.

Against them charged Lakota, Hunkpapa, Cheynne, Blackfeet. Sailing arrows migrated across the clouds; the air was peppered by muskets and shotguns and torn by the periodic conduction of howitzers that digested men's howls in their vortex, the armies wedded on each other's destruction, dancers wanting to come undone.

They chased them to the village. Spilling out ammunition on hundreds of thin-ribbed dogs, burning the tipis and awaking an extravagant blaze that turned the night to noon, executing those who straggled behind. Before the week was finished the General summoned him and told him to go or he would shoot Les himself.

"I have my suspicions about you, and out here I take my hunches for stark proof. You belong in a grave than a prison. And the reason I'm letting you off is because I belong in that grave neighboring yours."

He rode east a ways. He found a job repairing boots and selling watch chains. At nights sneaking to the town over and waiting among a cypress grove for a loner to come drifting by, falling on him and fleeing. Sometimes he roped them to the back of his saddle, the silhouette of a partner drunk asleep, and would cast it into the river. Until he got lazy and left them where they were killed.

He continued like that for a couple years, the chokings irregular but eventual, the relief they brought instant, pure, essential. Now and then he asked himself how he had come to need this, to value those seconds more than decades of life, and all he could think to answer was it had something to do with the instant when breath and life must cease.

In the late spring he leapt on one. The youth rolled out and flashed a Derringer from his heel and fired shots that missed Les by barely an inch, into the night the intent, deadly missives. Les went for his LeMat and sent the kid flat.

His stomach flourishing a rich wet whorl, he was not wholly dead; he could no longer speak, but he had not yet rid his final air.

Already men were running toward them and had reached him before he could think to flee. They looked stunned by this morbid presence. After a while blinking and catching his breath, Les approached the boy, leaning over him and inspecting him.

"Holy horseshoe, what this fella do?"

"He tried to shot me's what," said Les.

"What on earth you say to him?"

"I didn't say nothing. Guess I'm lucky he's a poor aim."

"This is been going on for three years. Men getting killed here this time of night. It wouldn't surprise me if this'n here's the one been doing it."

The boy's eyes cooling, lustrifying dull. He could sense the remnant of life speeding through his mouth and seeking the dark for those lungs in which it could hope to reside. He wanted to scream and shoo them away but half a dear minute, even to confess this poor child and welcome himself hung if only to reclaim the privacy—slipping, slipping, fading—instead of this marching band scattering the intimacy.

Over the corpse they gathered. Along with Les some were inspecting the body while others stood by confounded.

Les rose, let go his own exasperated sigh and broke from their crowd around the X in the middle of the street.

"Well," he said, "I hope I've taken care of that. I was just going along and out he sprang, firing his poor-aimed shots."

"Why this is Nathaniel Sight's boy!" said one.

"He's a sorry sight is what he is."

"Hell, he ain't been in town three days. Brought home a wife to show his pa and them."

Those around him had started to rise and study him like a group of rearing question marks. Les demanded he stay even.

"I ought to have spanked him," he said. "Spanked him and sent him home."

A few from the crowd chuckled.

"Got him a pretty wife he brought back home from out East. This sure's gonna ugly her pretty face."

"I ought to have switched him across my knee."

They stood around him, their attitude that of waiting to be dismissed. Then someone said, "I believe I found his gun."

"It's a little old fingerbone Derringer."

"Why hell! You don't go up against no man with no puny four-barrel Derringer!"

The words had not quite quit the air when he turned and began to run, the running the magic spell that worked to transfigure their speech to bullets. Upon him drenched a storm. He fled toward where he had tethered his horse. The whole town seemed to sprint outdoors and flood on him like a wave. He felt a pain dash up and nip his calf, figuring himself shot, but as he continued he understood it had only been a stone kicked up by a bullet.

So dark the cloudchoked night he could see no fire in his horse's eyes, the terrain over which they hastened neither land nor distance nor space but a terrorized suspension toward some safety unattainable. All through the night he could feel his pursuers behind him, their inevitable clasp grazing the skim of his back no matter how fast he whipped and beat them, but when dawn boiled over he found no one there but fields, no one behind him seeking his trail. Nothing but gray colossal plain.

For weeks he continued riding, loath to eat or halt. One night, daring a fire, he anticipated himself by taking a spit and ramming it into his calf. On the instant the fetor of searing skin. Almost passing out at the pain, though insisting he deny it not.

As a blind sun groped through the clouds, he envisaged himself forever on the run, always in the process of accruing a heap of new crimes that would eventuate his fall, yet beholden to their anchor, until they that had been seeking him caught up with him and then speeding to some place else where the cycle might again for a span resume. He knew he could not always go on living that way, the fear always hovering, prefiguring the cage wherein he would be made to bear his punishment. Trapped in a maelstrom that was his to control—the speed, direction, and power—he was aware that any hope of sundering lay in the hope of drowning.

Further, he grasped it had to do something with his service and the threat he had felt of being killed; then as he continued to probe the cause, he felt it somehow also linked with the memories of the life that was no longer his. But even had he seen the lucid diagram behind the labyrinthine reasoning, demonstrating how A grew into B grew into C, which equaled the insane D, still, he came to believe, he would never be able to say, Yes, yes, that accounts for it indeed.

It was then that out of the plains, like an artifact lost or thrown away and preserved indefinitely on account of its having been lost, he beheld Utica.

Spurring his horse through the monumental gate, what he saw was a town neither large nor small nor unique, but to his fitting. On the streets there were people who more or less looked like him. In their basic wants and needs and amiable indifference they could have been vaguely related somehow, as if behind a sanctuary of a thousand mirrors his true self might hide disguised, in return for which refuge he would vow to lead an acceptable existence.

7

"You calling it a day?" says George.

From his cell in the corner I can nearly make out Old Ruckus, who is eying me. He has been waiting for me to leave ever since I first led him in, waiting for the night to bring the quiet in which he can try to begin to get used to the place, become acquainted with his luck. And in fact I notice them both eying me: they are like two lovers whose piercing stare voices the heat in their tongue and that only your leaving can free, and they hate you for holding them back so.

"You've had a hell of a big day," says George. "You go on home and get you some rest. I'll close up shop. You just go on home and rest. And you come in late tomorrow. I won't snitch on you to no one."

"Well, goodnight," I say, snatching my hat from the hall tree, my footsteps and I in dialogue.

Ahead of me lies the door and all its openness, but before I can barely start to go to it I hear him singing out behind me, "What you doing tonight, Sheriff?"

For a few breaths I dare not turn; both of them are staring hard after me, I know. I can feel the hot imprint of both of them branding my shoulders, and it is that cagey, amorous fear that has made them conspire to want me out the door, and indeed I can smell it, the sweat from their lust after seeing me, the room quiet without me, my odor lingering a bit, then gone.

"He's just nervous about sleeping in the cell is all," says George. "Ain't you, Old Ruckus?"

"You're damn right I'm nervous," he says. "Not nervous, scared. Not scared, no. I'm pant-messing scared and—"

"Mortified."

"Yeah, that's the ticket. And I know I ain't the first to admit it's a cursed cell, and a cursed cell for someone's angling. I don't want to wake up tomorrow finding myself hung. I still gotta get me my lawyer and my fair trial and in the meantime take kind trouble not to get myself good and hung in this old flea-ridden bin."

Now he approaches the bars, so far as his chains will allow, that sound the rattling of too many crimes. His form is thin but rugged, reliably taut and strong, the way you would call a rope thin while admitting the rope is sturdy.

He leans forward blanketed among the shadows, someone who knows neither a people nor a country, a certain loneliness that out of which has grown much like a flower out of manure a particular sense of security that feeds on the fear and on being alone. He does not know that this discloses a vulnerability, which gives him a slatternly poise.

Outside beyond the door, the evening is cool and still, but I can feel a dark wind rising, anxious to carry us off.

"Good night," it comes as a grunt, "you two be good," and enter it, the cool, still dusk, I realize, nothing but a sign of the rising wind.

Just as you can hear a train cry some miles before it enters your vision or taste in the back of your spit a semblance of the fever that will lay you in bed for weeks, so I know the dark wind has been rising toward me from somewhere deep inside my future, across the years that are to come. The wind blows silent as it continues to well and build, and only once it has passed, in the exiting whisper, can you finally begin to hear it, perceive that such a wind has come, though gone.

As I turn the corner I hear George saying in that firm, placid lilt of his, "Don't you do nothing stupid and I'm sure you'll be all right."

Outside people's chimneys are smoking and all the windows are afire; I can see them farther on down the road and yonder to the hills, little warm pools with people drifting in and out the bottoms of them until they go merging with the stars.

I pass the crowd at Marvin's, but I decide not to stop in where folks can see me. What with the wind beginning to build, making the thoughts frantic and lifting toward it as it readies, I fear I should expose myself than lend support, for I don't feel much like talking business, and I assume these weary legs are taking me straight home.

Nearly out of reach I hear an explosion of laughter come bursting out of Marvin's, and suddenly I am seized by the paralyzing thought that something indeed could happen tonight—something could go horribly wrong—that someone would need me after some small disaster and would come around looking for me and find me. So I say a silent charm to whatever it is that ensures these things: "Let peace prevail so we can sleep."

Once inside and still a little curious about where these legs are leading me, like a father directed by a child's caprice, I find myself stopped and seated at the table, only myself and the gelid dark.

Am I to be patient or try and fight it?

I know there are no just means of stopping it, that once it chooses like a wave of mammoth portions, it is to break and topple me, and to prove resistant—to dare to try and fight—would splinter me like a clay rock from a slingshot, and therefore the best course of action is to be taken and to surrender.

So strong it comes I am almost got up out of my chair, though demanding I must wait, for by morning it will all be done. The wind is rising good now, but to let it really take me I must hold to the seat of my chair and trust there is more to come that this wind prefigures, to be patient and not fight. I can read it all so clearly. Yet the reading is not enough; the pleasure of it lies in the reading and in the knowing you will soon lift up your eyes and find the reading really real, since if it were not to be then there would not have preceded the reading in the first place.

Even when enough dark has come that I can safely say that Marvin has booted out his topers to sleep it off menacing the streets, an offering should I want it, I find it difficult to rise for fear my standing should bid the wind recoil. Not only is my whole body stiff from the afternoon's tussle, but now I must demand the limbs go and achieve what is to be done, as though the blind child who was guiding me earlier has been swept loose from my grip and I must summon my collective reason not to veer off and go looking for her.

At last I reach the jail. I have changed clothes and donned a weird bowler lest someone recognize my shape out lurking. Having met no one in the streets and hearing only my gait's whisper, I sight the mouth of the jail. Though the door is locked, it could well be open, for the aperture is wide and ominous as a corpse. Like the portal of a cave wherein a bear and her cubs are awaiting the intrusion that should bring them feed for the winter.

My key fits true, and now the door swings open, exhaling a humid breath with portents of the end and the warm bitter stale, and such a wind begins mixing with the wind of the night pouring in behind me, but then I think that maybe they could be waiting for me in there, inside. I have run out my luck years ago and in the meantime have been riding my luck's phantom. They could be waiting for me, tucked in the folds and crevices of the shadows, their veins as alive with blood as mine, but only mine real for the moment.

I go toward the lamp that I know is on George's desk, my heels in dialogue with myself, until I hear, "Who's there?"

Blinding about for the matches, I can feel him wait, the whole air stiff and clutched in rearing suspension, like a wave wanting to fall. I can almost feel the breath come lave against my cheek. I wait for the air to shatter when I answer him, and the voice doesn't know whether to call out again to something he wishes were simply his imagination: he is torn between wishing he were crazy and wishing he isn't.

The match explodes the dark. On lighting the lamp I drop it into the mouth of my boot where it burns a few seconds. The sting continues to bite well after the matchhead has cooled.

"Who's there?" he whispers again.

Now I carry the lamp over with me, but before I let him see what I am I hear him huffing, his fear total and incommensurate. It strikes me as a little bit funny.

"Old Ruckus," I say, not trying to stifle my laughter. I skip forward, sure I appear rather amenable.

"Sheriff. You stole back in to kill me, ain't you? Or how about I get me my lawyer and my fair trial, or you forget?"

Each claim to a voice so intimate, so sincere, we cannot but be deliberate, theatrical.

"Why now, Ruckus." I throw back the cell, aware I have total impunity, and seat myself as close as his chains will stretch, close beside him on the chill stone, aware I remain just beyond his reach with my gun. "That ain't no way to go about greeting a guest. Say, I been meaning to ask you, when's a boy like you turn from going by the name of Young Ruckus to going by the name of Old Ruckus? You ain't yet made nineteen, I'd bet. There ain't some kind of ceremony that goes along with apposites of age?"

I set my lamp off to the right and try to allow my eyes to accommodate the brightness, but the flame shines too painful to try to look at it straight on.

These old mismatched worn stones, scarred with tallies of days, tattoos of hopeful guilt, as though time and expectation could be rendered into a simple figure, their rough-hewn faces glossy with sweat. There is nothing in the world or no one I know better. Their mute, gray faces gaze on us in happy recognition as if we were seated among friends; Old Ruckus now is sniffling.

"I told that fella—I told him we ought to bypass Utica, but he just had to post his aunt a letter. Dumb son of a bitch. I didn't bank on no one spotting us. I allow you that, Sheriff. You sure can spot yourself a face."

"Why, Ruckus." I almost want to grab him by the scruff of the neck and tousle his hair. "I know the wanted posters better than the stink of my own pecker."

Cheered at this, he grins.

"Why hell, Sheriff, I didn't make you for a—"

At that I grab him by the throat, trapping it, and hit him once in the gut, forcing what's left of the wind to gush forth from his stomach where it swells up in his gullet. Then I hit his cheek too hard for I hear a tooth go loose, and I follow it with a jab to his nose, jumping up to my feet. For a while I have sensed the wind rising toward me—it may be rising toward me now, this instant, the wind of his final being—but because I have yet to feel it come brushing against my cheek I know that it could be upon me this very second if I allowed it to, is or is getting ready to.

His eyes are sharp, tight points, sharp with anger and horror and desire, an event they cannot believe sight permits. Weakly he lashes out, struggling for my gun. I desist for a second, long enough so I can smash his hand.

"Don't spoil it," I say. "Look here."

And indeed he looks me eye to eye. I can tell he is hoping that if he does just what I want I will somehow decide to take pity and agree he is fit to live and therefore somehow fit for entrusting any further commands I may have for him.

Bare-gurgling-noise indents the space. It is as he flails like a garment on a clothesline that I notice his sight starting to flag, the original terror beginning to ebb and merge to a seductive flow of opiatelike invitation, a welcoming of the quiet that gently awaits. And now more and more of him is wishing not to fight but greet it, to welcome it, this stranger, all of me strained toward this mounting moment, toward that second's beautiful snap, his edge blunting harder and harder.

Then it is gone—truly I can say it is gone.

I wait for a while, to be sure. My whole body quaking. Legs dancing where they stay. For I comprehend the wind is arrived, to appear on my summons. Trembling, I release the grip.

Then it trickles, that final cache of wind, the same one that has been waiting ever anxious, like a child squeezing itself and whining because he is at the utmost verge of letting flow, since I trapped it there some time ago, now gently becomes released, lingers there at the sill, as though second-guessing its good intention, before rising and continuing and venturing into the dark and lending itself unto mine. That stale acerbic foul is pure Old Ruckus.

I let him slump against the bench. His blunt gaze peers up chary and mistrustful, yet also a little more friendly where earlier it would have locked grips with a butterfly, now fragile, willing to be broke, watches me roll back my sleeve as I straddle the lamp close to scalding and add a mark with the knife. At first the blood hangs back almost timid, reluctant to venture forth; perhaps it is embarrassed it must expose itself from the vein and go slipping wantonly along, to be buffeted by the bumps of offending others, like a virgin caught among whores. But with a little goading out it runs, leaking dark and red and beautiful, the running of this lone tear.

When I finish, I dab it with my shirt, and I then turn to Old Ruckus and wipe the blood around his mouth. Then I remove his belt and, propping him against the wall so he is standing but threating to lean, as if he is attempting to fight me even from death, I force him to hang himself in the place they always do. Then, certain that he will stay, I glance back, return, and straighten the air, then lock the cell as I left it and replace the lamp on the desk and twist out the flame.

Beyond me the night is brighter than I recall. Perhaps it is close to morning, though there could be lots of night left and the excitement merely worked to confuse me.

I was scared someone was following me during the walk to the jail. Yet now as I make the walk home I fear nothing. Should I be caught, my death would be only just; Death will savor my corpse so battened with sin. And should I continue on undetected, then I am lucky to have escaped. Either way, something inherent to justice has been set right again, has been balanced in the night.

Climbing the steps, I notice a nuisance hovering and catching with each step. Midway to the porch, balancing myself, I doff my boot and drop there in the dirt the burnt match from the jail.

Sleeping—a magnanimous deep rich sleep, that kind of sleep beyond all hint of thought or dreaming, self-annihilating in the manner that extinction must be, where you unite with the great blind infinity—when a knocking jolts me up. Like an unsuspecting brim it reels me, pitching and resisting, up to the plane of consciousness, jerks me to alien day.

I throw on my robe in which I stuff a pistol and knife, but already I know it is George Cilton that is seeking to tell me about last night.

And indeed there he stands.

That stern and sorry look of his blinding me or the light.

"Sorry to wake you after what I said," says George. I find myself feeling a little bit sorry for him.

"What is it, George?"

He wishes he could bite his tongue and swallow the velvety meat if but to keep him from making the words. Because in not saying means it cannot.

"It's just that." He sighs and tries once more. "They's another one gone and hung himself."

The day shines sharply in spite of the clouds. The clouds lie cluttered in the heavens, leading me to think that at such a height the sky is all but windless and still, for all the wind is down my throat. He does not know I am exhaling to him Old Ruckus this very instant, as part of our dialogue; I am speaking his breath in his face.

"You saying . . . Old Ruckus is dead?"

Both of us waiting for the other to offer something that will, as it were, tie a ribbon on it and render this present acceptable, to share some common sentiment to help us steady the fluster.

Behind him people go about their business. Well aware that if I told him, "Yes, yes, I did it, I murdered the fellow just like the thirty-five other bastards that have tended to slip through your fingers, that you must let lie and dismiss," the people drifting behind would suddenly snap to and quicken, become substantial on account of the words, the massive necessity fixing them to the ground, their airy figments of unimportance turned real, now made things to render justice.

At the jail everything remains as it was. Finding him hanging in there again, I almost want to hold everything and rush to shake his hand in the hope of reviving him full of warmth and ready to go, like a friend who lived long ago or monument that I the owner of and maker must get my likeness of standing next to.

George watches me do my looking. Against which I notice I am fumbling, so I set down my hat and try to figure my best scowl of seriousness, unsurprise. Going to the spot where I left him last night, I see the cell door thrown back.

"I can't stomach talk of a jail cell being called cursed."

The stare, though pointed at a target beyond us, regardless works to accuse me. The stare is a language that I alone can read: while aiming it oblique, he is pointing it straight at my brain. It is a compass pointing you east but one that nevertheless guides you north.

In the air outside I can feel George's thinking, his fumbling for that ribbon that will hang it all together. If I don't say something he just might.

"I guess he figured he was gonna hang anyways. Killing them folks upstate and all. I guess he went for a private ceremony rather than make it a public affair."

George's steps draw him near me, so near I can begin to feel the heat. He stops out of my sight. His heat prickles the hairs on my neck, sending a silly shiver up my spin, his shadow coloring Old Ruckus's stare.

"You know, just wanted to rid himself of the world quick as he could."

"Right," says George, "but Old Ruckus didn't want to hang. You heard him say so last night yourself. Why when I left him he was knocking his knees. Our cell has a strange reputation he didn't want to take no part of."

Now George breaks away, a boldness to his steps that evinces a certain conviction. He has arrived early to work this morning for the purpose of reverencing him with that unquestioning confidence of the faithful at a shrine.

"He's got bruises on his cheek and on his hand that I'm sure weren't there yesterday, even after you wrangled him.

And look, there's blood pooled round his nose, all in his mustache."

Listening but not listening, I make it seem I am inspecting every point George has to offer, evaluating and judging it, determining relevance for worth. I weigh each fact in my brain, lobe against lobe, for I am the cynosure of brave, but all the while I am only biding my next phrase, hoping my brain will rid itself of the fog.

"Okay, I do see what you mean. I'm just not one hundred percent convinced why those bruises weren't incurred when he was hanging himself. Couldn't the boy've slipped a few times when he was hitching his belt?"

"Yeah," says George, "but look at this."

His heels clip off tartly, demanding I follow.

Eager to breathe the wide outdoors, to rid myself of the stare that works within my words, which staid there in the cell secretes the same miasma of a plain piled high with corpses and left to rot out the weeks. Together we stop at his desk. I search it, uneasy by what I fail to find.

"What?"

"My lamp," says George.

"Your lamp?"

"It's on your desk, not mine. When I left it at the end of last night I saw it sitting on mine."

"Huh," I manage to grunt. "That's mighty interesting. You're sure it wasn't on mine?"

I can tell he is uneasy; he is no longer looking me eye to eye, and he is swallowing a lot: he is trying to choke down the argument he knows he must vomit forth.

"As sure as sure can be," says George.

Paralyzed, my brain a startled fawn forgetting how to work its legs, together we two just stay there, each studying the other but not looking, flummoxed about where and when to go, what the object of this game must be. Maybe the words will find themselves.

"Are you telling me we need to investigate this for a homicide? Is that what you're saying must have happened?"

George continues to swallow, his gaze lost in the ground that is demanding he must hush. Finally he waggles his head, action under thought.

"No, I don't think so, Les," says George.

"Well then, okay."

I clasp my hands, but aware that George is yet enthralled in his mimic of the dead, as if the closer he stands to the boy the more he can infer the indictment.

"I guess we'll just concede Old Ruckus moved your lamp by telepathy." I laugh. The laugh runs a little too long. I go and take back the lamp.

After a while George breaks from his stare and goes and joins our business for the day.

8

Clouds marshaled in immense ranks palled the end of day. Turning their backs on the indifferent dusk, they went in a tavern called The Crossing Place. In contrast to the vast absence of the plain, inside an uproar, the volume and frenzy of which seemed to exist in an illicit state, dwelt like so many revelrous bears in a cave.

The uric stench of beer or spew or both urged on their thirst as they scouted an opening among the benches, the rollicking crowd waving a fixed-tiered sea. Men with layered beards—mustaches that had been cultivated and then renounced for mustaches along with hedges that in turn were forsaken for full-out beards—threw back their hats and roared, exposing a trove of septic teeth. Whores with squinting cleavages sauntered by pandering their fleshy bouquets. Someone was playing a rabid piano, music strangled of any melody and left to totter home in offensive drunkenness.

"Here's our place!" sang Quinn. Wending among curious who as soon as spotting it became engrossed in that foul eye.

The kitchen had run out of meat, so instead they ordered turnip greens and fried eggs that arrived confettied with cheese.

"They serving us sides for mains!" he hollered, his voice containing the scowl.

After drinking a little whiskey, they splurged for a bottle, their voices growing bolder where minutes before they'd hung back.

"I've been riding my ass off these weeks," said Edward, "which means tonight I'm gonna drink bottomless."

They looked at him, both mouthfuls agog—their bloated eyes met—and spat: hilarity shot past their teeth. People were pointing at them and giggling in this lunatic contagion. The twins watching each other, surmounting wilder heights, like a madman in dialogue with his jeering reflection.

Finally they began to subside, still heaving and gripping the table as though the next wisecrack might burst them clear away.

"That was a joke now, wasn't it? Wasn't it?"

"It wasn't supposed to be that funny."

"Say, where'd you learn a quip like that?"

"Yeah, you ain't told us what all you done after the war."

"We thought you was dead."

"And almost killed you a second time. We'd have to find us another stubstitute brother!"

In Edward's face that calm severity of a mountain when viewed from a safe distance.

Then he said to their surprise, "I was teaching Latin out East."

"Latin?" yelled Quinn. "Where the hell'd you get the Latin from?"

"Picked it up. I guess I didn't mean to."

"Shoot, the only thing I ever picked up to unmeaning was a damn case of the clap!"

He was grinning out the good eye, the other a gross inferno. His twin just shook his head, amazed but not really, his aspect fully admitting he expected to have the same conversation a week hence, at which point his brother would then be lacking a leg or arm or be living but disemboweled, even more run to the ground, dauntless yet and blithe.

"Go on and say something in Latin," said Irving.

They watched him decide which among the Latinstuff he should express.

"Nec prorsum vitam ducendo demimus hilum
Tempore de mortis nec delibare valemus."

What they heard sounded another brother, and for some reason it silenced them—perhaps not only because he had uttered a different tongue but because his knowing another language somehow implied he grasped something about them that they themselves did not comprehend.

"What's that mean?"

"You got me," said Edward. "It's a language that even when you catch what the words mean doesn't mean you catch the gist."

They looked at him, expressions in the way that if he had told them his mule had foaled.

"If that was me I'd make it up all the same," said Quinn. "Teach them whatever I wanted."

"You pretty much have to do that to a degree as a Latinist."

"So what was it like in the war?"

Something inside him gave a little, collapsed. That cool severity now unbecoming and sad. After thinking on it for a span, he took a deep breath.

"Wretched, to say the least. Though I'm sure you wished at times you were off there fighting, believe me when I say you were extraordinarily fortunate to have missed it. War is, well, atrocious. No, atrocious isn't strong enough. No word could begin to do justice to it. I've watched the corpses of my friends find burial in the bellies of pigs and dogs. I have tried to forget that, but somehow I can't seem to manage to."

He took a sip of whiskey.

"And that's where you lost the arm?" asked Irv.

"That's right."

"So I guess it's fit to reckon you ain't got no woman or kiddies there back home out East we should assume know about? No little chaps you was teaching your made-up language to when you wasn't making it to the missus out East."

Further down the bench somebody dropped a glass, a kind of alarm for him to regather himself, sit up from where he slumped. With a covert finger he pushed his glass beyond reach.

"I married, but we never had children," he said. "And that at least not for a while till I know how to settle down. Are you? Tell me you got twin pretty dames crying into their handkerchiefs right now, knitting their woes by the yard?"

"Shoot! Married? Married! Been married! Been?" said Quinn. "What, she run off for a bigger pecker and leave you off fiddling all by your lonesome?"

"No. The wife I had—she died."

"Oh," said Irving. "Our apologies."

"No, it's all right. I mean, I didn't marry right. I mean, I didn't let my brain decide things then but other stuff. Do you know what I mean?"

Intrigued they were by watching him piece together his thoughts, his pronouncements having the ring of truth.

"I expect some day I'll do it over again. Some day a long day off. Only that time I aim to do it right."

"Yep," said Irving, "women sure are something."

Quinn glanced around, turning his eye like a crazy hawk.

"Yeah, but take care you remember: they're not like you and I. Women themselves are different."

"And I'm all for splitting that difference!" Quinn chimed. "Split her in half like a fish out to dry! So long as she knows what's good and doesn't take to meddling. Last thing I need's a meddler."

Edward gave him an amiable jolt on the shoulder that was meant to recall him from some dream.

"You take it from me, little brother. A woman will quit to meddling no sooner than she'll quit to telling lies, and believing those lies too."

"Just let em lie, I say," said Irving rather aloof.

"Oh, I'm gonna let em lie all right. We gonna lie all night long!"

"A woman meddles in my business," Irv went on, musing, "you can bet she's gonna get a bust in the mouth. She won't meddle with mine and not receive her comeuppance."

"Oh, she's gonna receive her comeuppance all right!"

The socket, black and puffy, a dreary lunula like a moon behind an irregular cloud, oozed a sebaceous goo the consistency of snot that he kept wiping on his cuff. Both of them had been staring at him, with Quinn apparently welcoming the attention, unaware of what he owed it to. Edward thought about insisting he see a doctor, but then thought the better of it.

"I thought you and Pa joined up together?"

"Yeah, I thought so too until he ditched me when we were in town. He gave me ten dollars to provide for me and told me I had to wait a few days so as we wouldn't make the same company."

"How come he done that?" said Irving.

"I don't have a clue. I guess he didn't want to worry about watching me die or looking after me when things got rough. That or wanted his freedom. I ponder it a good bit."

The three of them were studying the ladies move from table to table. They were greeting potential customers, conversing with the rumps of their chests, which they bore like the beginning of a secret. As the chosen were led upstairs, they left behind them a commingling of admiration and hate.

Quinn swore and shook his head. "Shoot, some fellas got all the luck."

"They'll be springing a leak in the morning."

"*Suave mari magno turbantibus aequora ventis*
E terra magnum alterius spectare laborem."

"You stole the words right out of my mouth," said Quinn.

"I've been meaning to ask you fellas," began Edward.

"How'd we make out with Uncle Gruhn?"

"Yes, that's exactly what I was going to say." But now that they had embarked, he feigned indifference.

"He was a hard some bitch, Uncle Gruhn," said Quinn. "He wasn't easy. Maybe on hitting him you'd come to bust ope some good. Gruhn's a kindly old nut waiting to be broke ope."

"Hard to the point of fair."

"Why sure, he never like to've whipped us without being afterward a little hangdog. Pouting and all how it hurt him more than us."

"Ha!"

"No, we're kidding," said Quinn. "The bastard done whipped the farts out us and done it without thinking pat."

"He was a hard old bastard, but, you know, he done that for our best."

"But still," said Edward, stammering, trying to fit feelings to thoughts. "I heard such terrible stories. He didn't like, you know, do real bad to you and Mother? When Pa and I were working he'd just go on and on about how wicked he was, Uncle Gruhn. Stories he knew from the past. If I think about them for even a second it makes my skin want to leap right off. He never, you know, like slept with her? Uncle Gruhn and Ma?"

"Siblings sleep together all the time," said Irving.

"We don't, but they do: others."

"Yeah, but . . . I heard such horrendous stories, really deviant beyond belief. It's not right the two of them living together, don't you agree?" In his brow a crucial pleading. The twins stared at him their replicated astonishment, their same thought crisscrossed, tangled, but then, as if to burn the knot, one of them said, "If he ever ploughed her, he ain't done it in front of us," and Edward watched them giggle like girls at a sneeze in a sewing circle and decided to abandon the subject for the present.

By now the commotion in the bar was overwhelming—dozens on dozens of voices talking over themselves and louder, what must terrorize the minds of the mad. You had to shout and cup your hands in order to have any hope of being heard, the words swept into the cacophony before yelled. He felt restless, though neither wanting to leave nor return nor continue on the road ahead. In the uproar he watched their mouths wage an argument with him at the center, Irving asking and Quinn batting him off.

"Tell me what?" said the elder.

Quinn leaned forward. He wiped more pus on his sleeve.

"You wouldn't hold it against a fella for trusting his older brother?"

Edward tried emulating his smile.

"Why? What's the big old secret?"

"After him there's no one else I trust," said Irving, which sounded sympathetic enough. "But then lots of folks I trust broke ope to show no good. We need us kind of a test."

"And what is this regarding?" said Edward.

At that moment a woman cast up from the crowd and caught their table. Like the others navigating the tables, her chest was vamped and below the rim of her dress an expression of stuporous surprise seemed to lie in wait. When she caught sight of Quinn her easy air fled like a thing of wind.

"Lordy," she said, "what in Murdoch's mercy happened to your eyeball? Horse kicked you in pretty good?"

"It just seen something it ain't supposed to. Not no angel like yourself."

He grabbed her; she fought his wrist.

"I'm the angel's gonna black your other eye and whatever else's rolling."

"I hope your privates are sweet as your talk!"

Glancing at Edward for some sympathetic buoy, she was trying to pry Quinn's fingers loose until something inside her caved and she relented to his lap.

"What you say for cutting us a deal? How bout two for the price of one? I bet you ain't never been doubly wanted before."

"Old Celeste's been a lot of things, and shaking up with no dead eye ain't much on my to-do. Why you'll be humping me into my nightmares!"

"What?" said Quinn. The good eye was rolling as if hoping to catch the words that had flown past.

"How about three for the price of two?" said Irving.

At that Edward started. He shook his head faintly, but where she alone could see.

"And we don't want no yankees in the stable!" Quinn rattled her. "We're talking good clean paddling smush!"

"Boy, if you ain't some kind of cute," she said, regarding Edward, then lingering on his crotch. "But boy, if you ain't awful sad. Can you get him up so weepy? I'll take that deal so he'll quit playing lover's funeral. I say we'll bury something so you can get her off your mind."

They followed her upstairs, where the clamor began to hang back, the yells and howls now almost an imitation of quiet; at the same time, however, sounds they had been hearing, and which had blended with the uproar as a far compliment, peeled apart and became separate—a trickle of bedsprings and pleasure—like a leak disturbing the absence of noise.

They huddled before the threshold, none of them wanting to seem so bold in assuming his was first.

"No, no, you first, brother, you."

"After you, Eddie."

He sighed, feigning indifference.

"This better be one damn exceptional secret, with me risking my personal health and all to hear it pray told."

"You relax, big brother," said Quinn. "You'll back out clean. Only thanking us for the ride."

"And whatever the secret, I am *not* carrying a pistol. At this point I'd rather be shot than carry a loaded cannon."

"What about for all the gold your old mule can tote?"

He reined back where he stood, a part of him already laden with the spoils.

"I'll be damned if whatever it is is legal." Dread, foreboding, doubt, not wanting to let go his grip on himself, but already in this hesitating he understood he implicitly had.

"Shoot no, she ain't no legal!"

"But when the risk's this low, it's almost as well she is."

9

Once they discovered the farmhouse and the cave just beyond, a slight crevice tucked beside a thicket of aspens, they let Edward return to town, where he bought the lanterns, fuel, shovels, picks, and a burnished leather tote the size of a horse's barrel, bountiful enough to hold their grandest visions. Then they waited for night.

No one spoke. Each was laden with his own fantasy showing him mirific luxury so plenteous it could not but nip every desire long before the want had been accorded the chance to flourish—and the enemy who insisted there was naught. They waited as the shadows pooled to the sky, and then nothing was shadowed.

All lay quiet. Even the roiling of crickets punctuated by a marginal owl insisted a variation of quiet. From the far side of the hill they watched the smoke flow out of the chimney, and soon they scented dinner. After a while the light in the house went out.

They had tethered the horses and Edward's mule and now they divided the supplies. With a delicacy foreign to them, they tiptoed through the brake and quickly helped themselves into the cave. Irving went first and took the equipment. Followed by Quinn. Both having to steady their brother into the cave. Each of them held a lantern. Edward jostled out the matches he had bought. Impatient, they waited for him to strike one.

"I'm a sorry lefty," he offered.

"Here, I'll do it."

Adjusting the wicks, which were smoking, they treaded into the cave. The previous excitement now apprehension. The smell dank and iron and ancient like an old body filled with blood.

They hurled their lights against walls, and the walls sneered the conjoined teeth of centuries, a monstrous grin turned backward on themselves. Small noises ruptured loudly: the grind of their heals, infinite droplets, the flow of stream of unknown depth and whose current may have challenged a river, breath that came shedding the tincture of voice.

Sometimes he would stop and listen to his heart, a sound he had not paid much attention to for so long and that did not resemble him in the constant steady of it. Yet hearing the expected rhythm, he soon understood he held something essential he could not do without, the steady filling his sight and ears until the palpitations too became the quiet, all noises bleeding into each other, however slight and silent, making a quiet as shocking as strange, as inundating as familiar, the deeper they went down the cave.

"You said there's supposed to be an X somewhere?" His voice came back a strained tenor and went skittering off in the dark, fleeing any claim to identity, and raced abroad as nothing.

For a moment neither of them answered. As if answering might mean abetting, some corroborating of the dark.

"Ain't saying that."

They were washing their lights over every suggestive nook in hope of finding the mark.

"A guy we killed said so."

"He may've been lying," said Irving. "You know, biding he'd save his skin."

"Shoot, the bastard done that I'ma kill him all over again. Scared little some bitch wasting my time, trying to bargain with what he ain't got."

"I hope that's not the case," said Edward.

"Shoot, that's the case, then one day when I'm in hell sizing up the place, you can bet your ass that yellow bastard'll be the first damn soul I go a-seeking. Run a red-hot pitchfork right through his ass. Send him down to a worse hell he ain't figured to know was there."

Despite their three lanterns pooling together, the cave imposed its dark abundance against their flames, which rendered the impression not only that at any second the walls and ceiling might avalanche and extinguish their puny flames that did not so much stave off as antagonize the monstrous void but that they were traveling in a land defiant of comprehension.

"But then how'd he know the cave was here?" said Edward toward the ceiling. Looking at the lanterns' pained his eyes, and when he closed them they still stung.

"If that little some bitch was lying, shoot, I'm gonna go storm in and shoot them folks just for guilt in association."

"Oh I wouldn't do that."

"Oh I wouldn't? I'm gonna storm on in and say, 'You know that little pissed-pants skink of a fella that told us there was gold up yonder in that cave? Well, I'm awful sorry but I done went and blown his head off. And after you get through moaning about that, I'm the same right pissed-off fella that's gonna assume blow your heads off. Blow them off like candles right off a birthday cake. What you think about that?'"

"They're probably not even his parents."

"Hell," sniffed Quinn, "at that point I'm just gonna need to kill something."

They sensed they were cutting far beneath the hills. A land remote and spaceless and beyond earth and time. They were forced to wedge their way between crevices, had to suck in their stomachs so they could fit, cram past, or lie recumbent and push forward footly, scraping a ceiling the height of knees. Faint winds crept by, refreshing their faces, then the question arose: From whence did these winds come? Clambering up ledges slick with film from a spring that had been trickling longer than history. One twin scrabbled up, the other twin waiting, lifting Edward on his shoulders to the one who gathered him over. Each of them prayed the path would never split into multiple apertures that would then require they separate or spend days exploring a skein of directions, hunting a prize that did not exist.

The deeper they went, the more it confirmed they'd been duped. Having ventured this far in the cave, they may have been searching for several days, the sun rising and setting, qualifying a world that had forgotten them like a meal from yesterweek, and emerging bare of treasure would serve to constitute a world they could not approve, and thus they continued still. Their lanterns could have run dry, their voices wandered from their gullets, their footsteps groundless and mute as if hovering beyond nature, and all else save the fundamental volition directing them to keep seeking shucked, now absolute strangers to themselves, still they would crawl, continue. They shone their lanterns above, around, on everything. Doubtful they would see the mark and if they should they would not believe it, their eyes having become so steeped in doubt. The

light turning into this ambiguous, mistrustful thing, a phe-
nomenon as brief and unreal as the shadows spawned by
this bleary den of dreams. If they continued searching until they died, would that mean that they had died truly?
Advancing, flame by flame the fiery tears snuffing to extinction, then through a passage of uncharted days, led
by a slow mechanical trudge and tentative touch, the remnant will leading them forward, fingers, legs, flesh growing
wasted, boney, muricate, thoughts and threadworn brain
lost like the path on which they bellied, each in his turn
falling from the train (it could have been within seconds
or minutes of each other or weeks), spilling over to their
eternal resting place where no one would ever find them or
think they lay. Would being dead mean being so only for
those alive?

Vague scene up ahead. Professed in an open den of
sorts. Irving shone his light on a stark white X that someone had once marked over a sculpted-out ledge that was
fashioned to stairs.

"I don't believe it."

They stood before it, captive. The painted white mark
on the plinth its squinched eyes striving not to see. They
waited for everything to disappear any second.

Finally one of them killed the silence:

"We are going to be the richest sons of bitches in the
country. Won't be nothing left to buy."

The X a hypnotic object poised like a venerable shrine,
that to approach should connate such bold presumption—
even standing near seemed to infringe on blasphemy—
presumption to vex one's progeny, and what seed gen-
dered, the dregs wallowing in the sties of civilization, better
snuffed than perpetuate.

"I think we should—"

But before he could finish Edward watched his brothers race and flutter about the prize like moths avid for doom. He watched them lean into it, digging, pushing, cursing.

"It's giving way!"

"Yeah, I can feel it!"

"You pull!"

"I am pulling, dummy!"

"No, you're what's called pushing!"

"I pull, you push!"

"Yeah, you're awful keen on pulling!"

"We need your help, Old Stump!"

He watched the stone flirt with capitulating. A crevice of dark, somber light spilled out that compelled him to gesture frantically.

"Wait! Wait! Hold it! Hold it!"

The twins ignoring him, he rushed them, his lantern aflutter in their pursed faces.

"What? There someone coming?"

"Wait!" he said. "Just stop! Hold on for a damn second!"

They quit, their cheeks painted with clay, unbecoming in the harsh light. Before him they leaned, heeled like ravenous hounds.

"How the hell do we know it isn't daylight up there right now?" He spoke this at the tip of a hush. "That if it really does lead straight into Utica Bank, then how the hell do we know they're not up there open for business, walking round and waiting for us this second? Who's to say the second we bust right in the three of us won't get busted? We have to be slow and rational about this, fellas."

"We'll just tip our hats and make real sweet to them," said Quinn. "Tell them we're awful sorry we got the wrong address mixed up with another bank a cave over. Hope y'all don't much mind. Y'all have y'allselves a blessed day."

At that they recommenced shoving, straining. The marked block stolid, impassive, it seemed to inspire their primitive dance of desperation.

After watching them a while and beholding their nonsense, surrendering to a kind of irritable pity as much as to the possibility of a jailed fate, he marched up and joined them. He wedged his heels and began to push. Then suddenly he felt the block jog, and the three of them were guiding it toward the stairs that someone had evidently taken care of through his skillful design.

In the cavity above were the serried undersides of wooden planks. The planks were not new but neither were they dry nor rotten. They crouched there, grazing them with bashful fingers. Listening, straining to hear past the quiet. But nothing reached back from the other side.

"Hello!" Quinn pounded. "Money, you home? It's nine o'clock called quitting time! I hope you ain't gone to bed with that cheating bastard name of Poor Man!"

Edward sighed.

"What you reckon?" said Irving.

The elder pressed his hand against the planks, waiting to sense the thwart of some bolt or nut, yet all he felt was regular wood, and soon he heard himself saying, "Let's give her a good heft, and if she won't give we'll smash her on through. If we hear folks coming, you just turn and run and we'll meet a goodways down."

"Shoot, don't have to tell me twice."

After a three count they heft up. To their sheer surprise the planks wobbled loose, as though a fat man were stretched out on the opposite side, giving it his best to keep them from stealing through. On the next count the weight capitulated and the boards tumbled about; then each of them was standing waist-high in the work of their effraction, amid what they suspected must be a room.

The space smelled fresh, secure, intimate. A sterile purity to the dark. They could sense the pinpricks of hundreds of eyes busily scrutinizing them.

"Ouch," said Irving. He had reached out his hand and touched something hot. He ducked around their boots, catching the nearest lantern, which he raised up among them to shine against a room stuffed to the ceiling with gold. From the floor to the walls. From the walls to the ceiling. A room made of nothing but bricks of gold except for the hole where they had scattered the splendid neatness.

The light from the lantern flowered in every ingot so that it seemed they had come before the god who had incited their every desire, and these the desires now manifest, they stood transfixed in a mystic vision of fulfillment.

Again Irving ventured out his hand and touched a bar almost at random.

"They's a matter more cold," he laughed.

Hearing his voice fretted on the profane: as in a dream in which any verbal acknowledgement of the pleasure serves to recall the sleeper to consciousness, so here speaking threatened to shatter the bliss.

The three of them choked in silence, riches beyond imagining. Deferent, ecstatic, rapt, they stood there arrested with awe.

As they began to load it as fast as amazement permitted,

two problems quickly became evident: first, the leather tote would not hold even half of all the gold, and second, with the tote packed to the brim it was impossible to carry it back the length of the cave. At best they would have to store the gold out of the way until they returned and managed it out bit by bit.

"Where to start to buy with it all? A bigass house, a dozen Thoroughbreds. A wife for each color hair. I reckon I'll just be stuck studying it all the time, figuring out what to spend it on."

"You give your share to me. I can think of a million uses for every penny. You're gonna need to tie my hands just to keep me from buying the world."

"I'd be reluctant to flash any of these beauties within a month's hard ride of this robbed bank," said Edward. Then his frown became a smile. "But breaking my ingots into change is sure a trouble I'll enjoy fretting with."

The reverence and solicitousness now having given way to haste, they stacked the remaining ingots as though the neat uniformity of them might mask their depleted state.

It was agreed they would come back in a week and try to rid the vault of the last of them. For the interim they shoved the tote deeper inside the cave, in a shadowy grotto behind a prison of stalactites, where the bag assumed a guise beyond casual detection.

Then sifting back the boards, they shoved back the stone block where it had waited these unknown years for whatever original purpose the night had undermined.

For now they agreed they would take nine ingots to divide among themselves, which were not to be shown to anyone on pain of losing his share, or spent quite yet, but serve as palpable reminders of everything that waited.

10

Over the past few years I have increasingly found myself believing that George Cilton not only knows I killed those thirty-six fellows that were brought into our jail but that I continue to think on them from time to time.

There was the Arapaho I hanged that never fought me. I can still behold him watching me come to call on him in the cell: a certain marvelous seriousness he had that never quite left, even when I showed him Death's great confinement, the way he deferred to my grip like we were talking about dice and bachelorhood or had I been the ultimate chief who ordered he make ready for the long dark journey, even after he'd gone on hanging the serene little pools of his snapping-turtle eyes inviting me and gentle. A bandit the name of the Whitney Kid: I dare say there were more freckles of a dustblown red about his neck and back and arms than stars to a summer sky, for truly that night I witnessed his soul shake off its cage, the terrible fight he put up, not wanting me to send it on home, and my walk back home then glimpsing it out in the open, startled yet but calm, moonstruck as a foal and stranger to its legs and deciding whether to give up hope of finding a route back to the flesh where it had been comfortable those sixteen years or continue the new eternity wandering. I remember the indelible scent of concentrated piss after a two-day chase without refreshment—he had wet himself in my grip—and at first being so scared and beyond myself because he had gone and done it right there on the sheets and on those same sheets

I was intending to hang him with, but then the odor having gone to my head, I suspected people would make sense of it how they would, and did. The grip of that Mexican fellow that for every curse in his filthy tongue capped it with a spitwad past which he grit his teeth and fought me, the mad strong struggling to subsist and the blood blooming thick and ringent, painting his grin like a rare flower born of the feminine tropics, his giant forearms the chases of cannons (he knocked a tooth loose down my throat), the blue budding through the swarthy brown as we two locked together, overfilling with my intent, then the sudden manner in which he sped so that he may as well have turned to a tapping on his shoulder and then the seepage of the rank breath welling out humid and safe, whispering me his aim. The Mankato Misfit; One-eyed Jake; that idiot, whatever his name was, that escaped hanging for raping those women upstate. And every time as I come near, feeling with mounting certainty that this will be the last and swearing never again to think of venturing it, the justice so adequately restored and this a brand-new beginning for me, and it vanished from any thought, having run out my luck years ago, a napping dog, this You I have been looking for and risked all to win are indeed the fulfillment of that which prods and goads and nags until I have staked it all yet again, waiting for the message to come and blow where I can taste it, to tell me it is absolute and final and that it is this You, the end I was looking for, destined . . . but as the exhalations grow thin and begin to lose their flavor and any permanence to the message I thought I may have sensed has crumbled in my hands like a mud doll, I know I must keep up the old game and persist until I find You truly, the final You that releases me.

That look of skewed absorption he casts at me during his daydreams: it must be he is watching them somehow through me. Through the spasms and the twitches my gaze makes as I recall them, my memory must be tapping out the scenes, detail by wild detail, allowing George to take in the spectacle secondhand, a perfect, or as good, translation. He is frightened by what he sees but too curious to look away. Only when I find him, his aloofness coping with the deed and something of his shock branding it for my own, does he realize he is fixed, has given up the secret, the façade of innocence and possibility now entirely useless like a charade that has been announced prior to its pantomime and ever to be forged out of the air from whence he has understood.

It is then I think how much I would like for George to be there when it is happening so he might know something of the satisfaction and savoring when he turns in besotted shame from having relished the rushinggoing and turns his hands upon the final: that wind, that weight, that certainty as he bears down on his grip, never so rich, exquisite as it is just at that final moment, trapping the breath within.

We are about to close for dinner when out of the noon lethargy Sid Witchger breaks up the street, his thirsty footsteps shouting we are needed. He seizes our sight like a revenant come from the grave.

Catching his breath on his knees, he says, his voice less voice than wind, "Safe's been robbed!"

The declaration short, curt, insane, it can be nothing but plain fact. We follow him to the bank.

There we find they are closed for the day and Francis McGriff in a fresh suit of mourning waiting for us, his bald monster of a head worrying the breeze like a pimple.

"Leslie, George."

"Sid told us about your safe," says George.

"I just can't believe my eyes. The end of days is upon me, lads. I had no other choice but to close as soon as I seen her robbed. Come and looky at what's not here. Someone in this county is a damn thief and a liar and richer than sin with mine."

He leads us through the colossal iron screen. The bank is small, younger than its grandeur would have you believe. The patchwork of tiles in which our marmoreal voices sound keener than they are transfigures us to rich men of a second.

"You got a key, Sid?"

"Got a key to the outside."

"Only Sid and I got keys," Francis informs me. "But only I got ones to the inner vaults."

"We're gonna have to bring you back for a line of questioning," says George. "Part of the pat routine."

"I got a million questions of my own need answering," says Francis.

"I was talking mainly to Sid." Who up through now has been looking pretty skittish, but then I cannot recall a time when he was never not so. Meekly he nods, bowing as he would welcome a kick to the rump.

"Oh, Sid ain't stolen a pencil," says Francis.

From a tedious collection of keys he selects the right one, and from a chain hid in his waistcoat he takes out the second. The vault clicks open and the solid door swings forward.

"Sid ain't dim," Francis calls back to us from the dark, "but he ain't the brightest nickel either. That's the mind I want from all my tellers: a bit overcast, but unmenacing of thunder."

Once in the vault a dusky light edifies a room chocked from floor to ceiling with safes brimming with stoic faces, each unlocked by individual keys and designed for the spate of settlers that arrived here thirty years ago because a gold nugget the size of a peach pit was discovered somewhere in a neighboring stream. Centered there in the room stands a final vault that about six or a seven people linking arms and sidling around could circumambulate in a game of ring-a-ring.

He brings us lamps from where they wait in the corner, ignites them, and doles them to me and George.

I can tell McGriff is frantic, but there is also a strange calm underlying his manner, since when you know you have lost something beyond important that you have no hope of ever regaining—that worry you have been so zealously guarding with self-consuming attention throughout every step of the day for years upon years awake and in dreams beyond dreams now suddenly rendered gone, as rid as a date in the past—life becomes rather adrift like a feather rolling in a lonesome plain.

We see him take out another key, this key on a silver leash, shiny in spite of the prevalent dim, and now match it with another key from the ring. The lockwork snaps to and he shoulders forth the vault: the air reaches us cool and stale and empty.

"Bring your lamps up, boys. You'll see just what I mean by a noticeable absence."

We step up into the vault, George and I. Behind us there is Sid who cannot quite bring himself to join us from whatever guilt he feels he must display, if but to exonerate himself of all those times he wished to do so.

Like a magician who works in dreams, McGriff gestures over the den, his lamp populating the dark with a realm of bullion.

"That's a lot of gristle," says George, his cow's face pop-eyed now and strained. "More than a deputy's pay."

Bounteously stacked and dormant, about knee-high, bars surround us. They are pristinely gorgeous. Perhaps it is the secrecy that seeps from the dark light, but as he shows them to us I get the sense they are particular to a vision we are not supposed to be seeing: the sleep of creatures hibernating for the winter whose sleep should be wholly unknown to sight.

"Looks like a lot," says Francis, "but it ain't. I tell you boys about half them gold's gone missing since last I studied them, and last I checked my gold ain't grown no legs."

"This is *your* gold?" says George.

We can hear Francis McGriff swallow, wishing the spit were courage he could give us the lie.

"Some of it's mine. Most of it's them Highland Row folks' along with some old Confederate reserve and whatnot."

"You sure no one else has got a set of keys?" says George. "You never lent a teller them while you was, say, out on a trip or something."

"I'm telling you," says McGriff, becoming incensed, "these keys accompany me everywhere. They're on my bedpost when I sleep; they're in my breast pocket when I'm on my knees on Sunday morning; they're in my pants when I'm sitting in the craphouse; hell, they're even at the rim of my gaze when I'm doing business amongst the missus. For someone else to have a set of them would be . . . downright impossible."

To reach a hand and, outside of the conscience of the lamp, deftly palm a bar as he feigns attention, to slip the bar inside his pocket where he should fear the weight of it might reveal the purloined figure and at the same instant plunge forward in having acted the ferocious lust, how he would cherish the robust spending of it, like a millstone around the neck of a martyr—I know that right now this is running through George's brain no matter if he only contents himself with simply running his lamp over them.

I tap my finger to the cheek of one. The chill for an instant causes my skin to melt until I rip my finger apart.

"Think Annie might take the key?"

Inside the dark I can feel George grimace. But as Francis is a man he has dissected the theft from every angle, the entry of his wife in the night being the main incision he has returned to and probed again and again: the lover she might have galloped off to meet, the outrage of her spurring his own horse toward him, his conqueror, the stolen bounty restricting, constraining, constricting the fundamental urgency, and at last the debased breath to work their dance upon. His face corroborates how I expected him to meet me.

"Hell, Sheriff, the gal's sore afraid of the dark, let alone to be out in the street and steal up here in the night. It would take an awful stash of moxie most women just ain't got, least of all my Annie."

After quitting the vault we press the lamps into the keyholes for clues of a forced entry, for signs the lockwork has been tampered with, but everything appears quite ordinary. No evidence of disrupture, no evidence there is theft. Indeed the gold might have left by its own accord, and the single answer I can think is that at some point in lost history the thief has gotten the keys; it may have been many years ago and the thief just bided his days, letting the crucial exchange sail father away in the pull of time's easy tradewind until slipped behind the offing, and so he has come here and done the deed right under McGriff's nose, that or McGriff stole the bullion himself. Whoever it is, I would be breaking for the other side of the world right now, heading for that place where they would know me for a rich man since the beginning and where my chief entertainment would be cutting my gold into cash and savoring the slow spending of it to keep me from being let onto.

"I don't reckon I can pay you boys to stay here and stand guard from whoever it is that's broke in. I'll let you in the lobby and you can camp out on the floor. Hell, I'll pay you x-amount of dollars a night for the next whole month: you name the price. I know Les has a fondness for metal. It ain't gold but silver's your monstrous hoard, ain't that so?"

"That's so."

The smile on his boiled head makes the bursting of him appear imminent.

"There's something smart about being sheriff," he says, "and leaving a stash of sterling in plain sight where any old fella can skip right in and take it if he dares. It's when they know you're wanting them to come, telling everybody with ears to hear, 'It's there; go on and take it if you dare,' they don't much care to come. Maybe if I'm sheriff no one will touch my metal. You boys got room for one more?"

He says that for the three of us to laugh. We do.

"So what'll it be?" says Francis. "I don't mind paying if it means protecting my investment from any more loss. I'd sure savor the prospect of catching the crafty some bitch that done it and figuring out just how he done it, but mostly seeing his damn gizzard hung."

"You can count me out," I say. "I got enough holds on my time."

"Well, suit yourself, Les. George?"

George wrinkles his brow. In the deliberating lines you can see how he is envisaging himself: alone here on the marble, shivering and bored, the sterile silence of it all, tossing for that huge silence and praying no one returns and if they should, then hoping the element of surprise may prove strong enough that he might overpower perhaps a gang. In that timeless wedge of night he is wishing he had company. Now and then he wonders about his wife at home with their four children and how she is bearing it, whether she is not awake herself and cussing him for leaving her alone in bed, if she understands he is doing this because of her.

"Okay," agrees George.

"That a boy," says Francis. "You be here for nine, and I'll meet you to let you in."

"Sure you don't want to lend me the key?" says George. "I can make a few dozen copies and auction them off on the steps."

He says this for the three of us to laugh. We do.

Back at home, after eating a simple dinner at Marvin's and standing a few spirits—as many as it takes to bury people's inveterate hatred of the law—I undress and lie on the bed.

The house is lifeless, like a shell without any pulse. On listening for something to come, I detect a trot clopping down Main, counting the hooves in pattern: hind, fore, hind, fore; right, right, left, left. There is a blue jay some houses yonder. There is a crazy male voice hollering that I will choose for the time to ignore. Then, after a while, they quiet and I can hear my own breath only, the timid welling followed by the bashful sigh. It starts kindling quicker the more I lean in and attend to it, keen beyond my instruction, and I remember Old Ruckus and chide myself that he might yet be there alive had I shown a bit more reserve.

There is no wind rising now, only my breath, though that does not mean it will not eventually (it might be months or years or decades until our cell has somebody new constrained, until I can match another sign to face, and then the wind will stir, a sign it has got to be, is coming). I think I have got to show more reserve from now on, have got to take more care, or else sooner or later they are bound to catch up with me. Had I withheld for just a while longer he might be there alive and waiting and I could enter the cell tonight. That last release of breath welling up so quiet and frail and tender, unlike anything I expected, as if he knew such a thing would please me. Those fighting, tremulous eyes terrified by what they knew they would not see once they blew. How gentle they became! How tender!

I grab the letter knife from where it rests on the bedside table, the bronze tongue wagging in my grasp, and wrench it into my calf: the pain sings like an angel. At first there is a small little tattletale of blood that creeps beyond safekeeping, easing toward my ankle. The sheen so dark and lustrous that were I a painter, truly I would paint every scene this color. The red goes dripping onto the bed.

I attempt to guide my quivering hand. The knife very much wants to stay. But after some prodding, I make it reclaim the handle and see how much farther I am able to draw down the blade. The coward calf splits to, revealing the dark liquid, the calf a stranger to its usual face. The sight makes me feel funny. It is like I am carrying around a monster who gurgles blood whenever he pleases and could be carrying him around wherever I go and nobody has the faintest idea. I admire the wealth with which the wound flows and how the blood collects on the bubbles tiny pearls of reflective irises, and indeed nothing else strikes me as so beautiful since beauty must be this and this alone. I am about to faint for the pain, but that is only because it must be, and indeed it seeks a way like justice.

Having wiped my hands in my hair, I take an old shirt and tear it to rags. I use these to sop up the red that is runneling down my leg onto the quilt. Odd footprints mark a tortured dance across the floor.

As I am cinching the fillets, I think the imprints re-semble a sort of animal caught in a trap and one who has foregone the captive leg for the price of its freedom. The image in my head forces me to stop. I burst out laughing.

It is nine o'clock. After spending the last hour hurrying door to door and frightening folks out their wits as they in the midst of readying for bed, finding me on their porch—the horrible shock of recognition—are instantly compelled to scrutiny their consciences to turn up the worst sin that should summon my presence at this hour and assuming that, even if they cannot remember, the terrible thing must certainly exist, because I know, am there and beckoning, my presence to confirm it fact, I have found what I was seeking, am running toward Utica Bank, the same steel image in my head since this afternoon urging me forward like laughter from a storm.

When I get there I am out of breath, my brain riant, light, and tippling.

I bang the door over and over. The night hangs thickly, my sweat becoming the fog, so thick you could slice it with a knife. I hear the door beginning to relent, the locks upsetting like a sick stomach, and then it opens on Francis McGriff and George pointing at me his Rogers and Spencer. I can feel the bullet wanting to plant itself in my brow and grow the flashing stalk.

"Why cut my corn, Sheriff," says a pale Francis. He looks at me for an obscenity. "Don't you have any idea what kind of time it is? I was about to kill over on account of your inspired heart attack."

George just continues looking at me; I can tell he is sensing some malfeasance. Though he had not thought of it before, now I can see him wondering if it is I that is behind everything, the one that has played invisible, and questioning whether he has strangely volunteered to guard the bank against myself, which I believe he would be reasonably glad to do and ascribe his defense to the blessed necessity of shooting me, which equally well scares him and freezes his blood, knowing that I would truly want that.

The three of us are standing there in the vein of lads whose hands have been caught in the cookie jar and that are at least grateful they will incur whatever punishment among the company of their coconspirators.

"My apologies," I say, sucking in vats of breath. "I thought . . . you know, well . . . my apologies."

Then they sling their lamps from roasting the sweat off my face to yonder and about, should there be someone more than myself. It takes them nearly a full minute to realize I am holding that something more, not just featured like this myself.

"Good gracious, Les," says George. "You going out trapping this late?"

"Yes, yes," I burst into laugher, "exactly! That's it exactly!"

The ridiculousness of it has claimed me puppet.

"Gentlemen, please just humor me."

11

For several years after the war there were spans where I couldn't bring myself to get out of bed: no matter if it was a holiday or if there was much urgent work to be done or if my welfare directly hinged upon my raising myself from the frame and throwing a few stale clothes on and walking the quarter mile to wherever they that might be seeking me needed me to come, for the life of me staying right there in the folds was all I was ever good for, all I could hope to do.

To the few who knew me I must have appeared a sort of recluse; to the fewer who glimpsed me they must have noted the dark and gloom I'd come to radiate, wherever I'd go my presence throwing a sorry blanket over a sun-filled room.

There were homes I got turned out of not so much because my indolence kept me from paying the rent but because too many times, having waited for me to emerge and when I didn't, having waited for the pad of my footsteps upstairs and not hearing them, after weeks of worrying and straining to catch a quick noise that might be a sign of some vitality, then coming and busting the door, they had been frightened to believing my corpse lay overhead. Yet none of them realized the act of buying a gun and blowing apart my brain or creeping downstairs to the kitchen in order to pilfer a knife and treading back up again dangled beyond the limit—that even pivoting on the ticking hurt for what it cost.

I forget how many jobs I got let go from and how many houses picked me up, sheets and everything, and dumped me around the corner until some other work, some other roof overhead, seemed to gather me up and dropped me hence.

During all those years the central thought I kept returning to: I can't keep doing this, can't keep going. Can't continue continuing. Just give me the ounce of strength to end it all this moment or give me the blessed cowardice to dupe myself into thinking it will all be momentously different. That idiotic fancy to trick myself into believing that help may lie around the bend so that at least I might be moving.

Beside one of those beds a previous tenant had left a grammar for a language I had never heard of or had any interest in learning. As if to verify what did not concern me, I thumbed through the moldering pages, expecting the crushing tedium to come bearing down at any second and demand I let fall the motive, put it down forever and forgotten. A bit amused that any human person would spend his efforts learning something that had long gone extinct and no one went around declaiming for any purpose, at that point I couldn't have known this grammar would prove the fulcrum for tipping my lethargy into deeds.

Little by little I memorized its chapters, the paradigms and words. I went from simple sentences of subject and verb to acquiring the prepositions, participles, and pronouns of adolescent intricacy that kept them extending, elaborate, expansive, no reason why I was forcing myself to undertake so esoteric a challenge, perhaps only to see if I could.

Next, I wanted to render something from that exhumed tongue into the worthwhile one of my own, and I chose a text at random, from which I began cracking a code that straddled nonsense and clunky meaning, watching my work merge from babble into compact thought. I have learned something, I heard me telling myself. Though what was learned may well be pointless and ridiculous and hardly worth the labor, nonetheless I do know something: an artifact from the folds of ancient history, which my tending and preserving may help keep yet alive, even though I myself am not worth such keeping.

Then I began teaching the sons and daughters of parents more deluded than I, since, whereas I had stumbled haphazard into the learning, they were intent on seeking it, a certain mastery of elitism by means of their bored children whom I was painfully, tediously killing with my language, had been instructed to instruct, rendering them as tired and dead and lifeless as I had once been, bent over their trapped desks like stubborn hinges turning out declension against declension, seeking that I should teach it that they might live by that which could hardly be called alive, a handful of cool embers warm enough to help none but the very coldest and bereft of any heat for those even passably tepid. Until all that lead to its own trouble.

Beside the horses we waited until dark, with us a larger tote newly burnished with a stiffness hard as board. The clouds swathing the moonglow to soft cream, we went jogging among the trees, tools and bag and steps shuffling in quiet haste, back to that chasm centered at the fold of earth and hill.

Going along as we did a week ago. Our path through total darkness familiar not for any physical route but for that dismal sense of cleaving a passage through the void, eternity threatening to swallow us whole. Feigned glimmers of light that when looked at straight on were never there.

Over some vague while we have gone from a fast walk to almost running, incited by fear or greed. The deeper we get the more we have become alien to ourselves, and every instant takes a great amount of focus for me to try to ignore this, to attempt to fight the mammoth temptation to snuff out our three wicks and surrender going neither backward nor forward but allow the endless dark to engulf us, body and mind, and take my bed here in the stomach of the cosmos and savor this hovering to the end of things.

Just as I am warming up to the idea that we will be delving farther and forever inside the cave, hurling beyond midnight and space, an impossible quiet save my brothers' trot stirring my head like a nest of hornets, we strike upon the X. All is as we seem to have left it.

"You better spend every penny," says Quinn. "Hoarding is worse than sin."

"Quinn," says Irv, "can you imagine? Each of us has more money than he'll know what to do with. I don't think in a million years I'll ever know what to spend mine on."

"I'm sure gonna savor beating you boys to see who wins fastest spender," he says.

We undo the overstuffed bag, and our hopes hinged to reality and fancy reveal they are one and the same. Each ingot waits where we last saw it, the luxurious gold the truest fiction for eyes, each exuding an innate light.

Only with the intrusion of remembering where we are does Quinn shut the overchoked bag, and the three of us pivot the X-marked plinth from the spot that someone at some point devised.

Again we knock the boards at the center. Again the cramped, rich den greets us beyond the most generous of welcomes.

"Looks like they brung us more," says Irv.

"Looks like they was kidding themselves we ain't rid them of none on the first round."

"Let's just go easy," I say.

"Shoot," says Quinn, "you're like a scared old woman afraid of salt and pepper. Then you stuff me with chili and you cuss me when it backfires."

We set about loading more gold, moving two or three ingots at a time. Each bar's tempting pulchritude makes it seem as though the weight were unessential, almost floating, yet when you reach and heft her, then you are reminded of so many of life's strange beauties that house inside them an adder or infidelity, which must inevitably go dead at your touch.

"Fellas, who's the real controllers of this bank?"

Cupped in the warmth of your palm, each gold bar turns from frigid to warm in seconds, as long as the steps it takes to select a bar and load it, each a kind of stony flesh. Then you put down the gold, and it is as cold as it was before.

Soon the second tote is crammed to the brim, and all the gold has been removed barring a dozen or so ingots that plead for us to steal them rather than leave them behind companionless, the insulting scraps for the dogs.

"Okay, ready?" I say.

Now Quinn ducks up. I can see he is carrying a pry bar. With his bad eye puffy like a turned-out hole, he appears intent if blind. Though I know precisely where he is aiming for, necessity calls me to ask him what he is doing.

"Fixing to see what's on the other side of that door, Stubs. You care to lent a hand?"

Irv perks up, pivots. I can tell he is startled by the thought that he and his twin have not shared. I wait to see if he will speak before I must.

"Quinn, I wouldn't do that if I was you," says Irving. "They might be a gang out there, surrounded us. They might be waiting for us to stick our neck out."

Which is sensible advice enough, but Quinn is already working the pry. The noise comes loud, obtrusive, arrogant. When the lock doesn't remit, he starts at mashing it. Spearing the lock with the pry so that both of us most cover our ears for the abrasive contusions. Something about his rude strikes jarring me to cringe as I well should, their thunder evocative of rape. Telling me he has a familiarity with rape. A life I will not ask him about.

Irv and I have edged toward the exit, expecting the dread fulcrum where our luck swings from good to bad. Finally Quinn desists.

"Looks like she ain't in the mood. Anyone else for taking his turn?"

Both of us remove our hands from our ears. I look at the twins: warped versions of one self, sweet mirroring sour. Quinn doesn't realize—or realizes but doesn't recognize—the extent to which he has enraged his brother.

"You goddamn idiot!" he screams. "Now you gone and done it! Now you woken the whole damn town! Now even if they don't come running this next minute, now they got your pry marks and know for sure we come from locked inside. Now who's to say they ain't for going down into the cave and finding our laid-by gold?"

Quinn's face, pensive, succumbing to rot, admits he had not thought of this. At once he too fears they might find our stash scarcely hidden a few feet off below, but what he says is, "You just call me idiot?"

To which I hear Irving rejoin: "Hell yeah I just called you idiot. You might be looking out a sick whore's snatch, but I know you got human ears."

And at that they begin to tussle. About us there is scarcely space for a henhouse. They switch stances flitting and holding each other as the other one tries to extract himself; they give the impression of fighters that want to embrace but don't know how to go about doing it.

"Don't call me idiot! You got that? You got that, little chap!"

"I'll call you what I want to call you! Dummy, idiot, jackass."

"Better call me Big Daddy! Better call me Big Daddy!"

Meanwhile I am working on pushing the bag, trying to drive it nearer toward the gap and into the cave, but the ingots are dead weight, amassed like murder to a good conscience.

Then I see the door swing open. The door parting a slight fissure, thereupon my stump goes for my gun, my gun which I do not have, while neither of them has ceased fighting. I hit the back of their head.

"Shhh!" I hiss. "Look over here."

Once they notice they disentangle themselves and aim their pistols there at the crevice, the silent wedge staring at us and challenging our nerves.

"You see anything?" says Quinn.

"It just went to."

"You think somebody opened her?" Irv whispers.

"Shhh," I say. "Just listen."

Our ears are narrowed on the quiet. Sifting that space for the tiniest glint of movement that may signify some feat propelled by man. After a while of hearing our own breathing, we learn that they are either more patient than we or we have spent these last minutes imposing on the silence a still volition.

"I'm going out," says Quinn. By his stance he means to go.

"I wouldn't do that," I say. "That bag's quite fit her limit."

"I don't care about no bag."

His good eye blinks at Irv.

"Yeah, I ain't going out there either."

"What, you both chickenlivered?"

"No. We both gonna split your shares when you get capped on your first squint."

"Oh, you gonna split my shares? Hell, they might be diamonds and rubies out there and more gold times eleven, and you boys ain't gonna have but a rind of my huge fortune when I get through with adding milk to my barrel. Hell, I'm gonna make my trade borrowing on y'all boys. Call me idiot. Shoot, you both gonna be calling y'allselves dumb idiot after I get through with staking my claim in this here land the name of Quinn."

He knows he has hit the mark, has struck the perfect combination of keys to effect the tune that will move his brother; you can read the change overcome his front.

"All right," his twin concedes.

"Now we talking, boy!"

"I'll leave the milk to the fledglings," I say.

"Your loss, Handsome."

A palm held up in testing, timid, he pushes the door, which swings to, light as if unhinged. Beyond them there is dark, a night beyond night. I wait for the void to enliven with lead, that rapid greeting of bullets, but it is just them and spaceless depth.

"After you." He turns to me and says, "Give me a lamp."

As I reach down for the lantern at my side I see Irving step down in my extreme vision—Quinn's sadistic grin distends in the blanching glow that erases his lesser features, leaving a pure, weird form, his skin the pallor of angels save the foul jettatura and cornelian goo: he appears to me the soul of himself, a better, beatific Quinn with whatever innate villainy sequestered to only that gross sink alone, the rest of his face the empty shape of a cast—then the peace is broke as from behind us we hear a rabid-merging-crunch and from under that grim noise Irving's flailing, his terrific terrified screams assaulting the void. If there is anyone within a mile of us he is now awake and knows us.

Thrown light on where he stands shows his foot caught in a huge bear trap.

"That ain't good," says Quinn. His expression the apex of relief, incredulous at his luck.

Irving, however, has transcended any sentiment but sheer pain. All he can do is scream and scream as if hoping to donate even a cent of it into the beggarly air. When I bolt over to have a look, he grabs my hair, an automatic clenching, as if he were attempting to offload a share of his torment.

"Quit!" I scream, fighting him. "Hold still!"

Prying the fierce, indefatigable jaws that do not so much budge while taking care among his kicks and spasms my fingers do not get caught. The teeth of the device have bitten deep to the root of its gums. I search for a pin or key. Quinn just beholds our frenzy.

"Who the hell is hunting bears in a damn bank?"

Then I hear the worst of possible noises—it makes my heart choke in my throat—worse than Irv's flailing and lunatic screams, a thousand times worse than the worst cuss you can strain your wit to think of, and that coupled with all the worst screams in hell.

Not far beyond us the insides of a door scrape and remit, thereupon releasing a stranger's voice that shatters the limits of the abyss.

"Hold it! You boys are under arrest!"

I hear the surefire draw of a gun.

"Not yet we ain't!" says Quinn.

He strides behind the vault; as for myself, I must somehow juggle bracing my flailing brother with trying to set him free.

And now the silence explodes itself. The air instantly heavies with powder. Bouncing shots wild off everywhere so that even when it halts a mute rage continues to explode like a wild horse screaming. Whoever it is that is shooting at us remains invisible as we remain nicely delineated by our light like frightened children around a campfire.

I scramble to the floor, in part to cower from being shot and also groping for Irv's dropped Remington that I find, and go edging back into the midst of the safe. All whoever it is has to do is skirt Quinn's blasts or wait until he must change cylinders then race around up front and we are open to getting shot.

"Throw her!" screams Quinn.

I throw him the Remington as bullets cleave the air and rebound off the vault.

"I ain't never much liked Sundays!" says Quinn.

During this gunfire Irving has not stopped his maniacal screaming, but at Quinn's approach he abruptly hushes, just sucks back short shocked breaths as shots recur (time and again I have watched them look at another, decide or finish each other's thoughts, which has led me to wonder if they share the same pulse, the same brain even). Yet something strange now occurs: Irving's tortured gaze is pale, thin, vulnerable, evoking the fear of a struck fawn, and there is a vulnerability to Quinn's as well, an urgent seeking akin to pleading, even underlying notes of apology, I detect, weird in that vacuum absent of all remorse.

Each is breathing the same breath, and before I can expect him to kneel and unloose the trap, like a miracle of fraternal love, he has shot him right in the brow.

"What are you doing!"

Still poised over while whatever stranger's shots still ring, he fires four more times from Irving's Remington:

BROOSH! BROOSH! BROOSH! BROOSH!

They have swallowed the earth in their callousness—a vicious blast that I wish would consume my hearing—scattering Irving's face on the cold bank floor in a whorl of skin, incondite blood.

"Grab a lamp!" he screams.

I knew something was bound to go wrong and yet I stayed, insisted, did.

My ruined brother behind us, we abandon him and leap down the gap, Quinn and me next, into the clear, calm dark, slipping like drunks across frozen water, and continue to run and heave.

Mustering the courage to glance behind, in my sight there is nothing for me to see but the X-marked plinth neither bidding us farewell nor seeking our return, rather the front of a dead man casting out from wherever he may be looking, where meeting that vacant stare does not insist a meeting has been ventured.

No one is chasing me now but my brother. He is running after and cursing my light that once thrown back exposes he is having a hard time of it; his legs are stiff and embarrassed, both of them seeming to grin gladly up at me, both of them alien and savage, two different evils combined in unified form, their weird admixture leaving them all the more remote from the ways of man. For me a sight to keep on running.

12

When I wake it must be around time for dinner, for I can hear the murmur of Marvin's customers come welling up through the floorboards, the words they holler garbled but clear in raucous intent. As these come welling, there is also a scratching at the window from the fir trees that thrash in the gusts. Their cryptic shadows thrash and fight to climb higher toward my stomach. With a particularly forceful gust they make it so far as my throat. Roseanne is reading a book in her rocker by the window.

For a while I watch her eyes stutter along the lines: they cast toward the door then repel again toward the window like ignorant bugs that knock and fling themselves to the vision of but not freedom. The pulse at the base of her throat, which seems to waver, remonstrates me for looking at it so long. It is of a naked soft cool warmth, a beauty alive and much too pretty to cherish or hope to enjoy.

In the room there are some straw chairs, a wardrobe whose mirror I know is yellow, then the washtable and brass bed.

"You're awake," she says, unlooking, the fir trees scratching at the window. "You sheriffs sure know how to get your share of shuteye."

I stretch, which causes a little groan.

"Maybe that's the main problem with all the world—not the evil folks breaking the law but the good folks sleeping too much who should be stopping them."

She says this not glancing up, her stare skipping along the page, forth and back, the casual breasts watching me, their dreary sag and overall visage pouting and squatly cynical as if having been sworn the only objects of men's devotion for so long by men who have forgotten them minutes later, with each new forsaking they have learned to distrust the world yet more and more until even the cynicism has had no choice but to exhaust itself, and then there is the looking at and envying the ground. Countless men waking here day after day, men much like myself.

I raise up from the bed.

"How could you tell?"

"How'd I tell what?" she says.

"How'd you know I was awake?"

"Just cause," she says. She pretends she is still reading.

"Cause how?" I say.

"Cause you weren't breathing and now you are."

How could she know I went to sleep this morning at sunup, that I watched her from the chair, pretending to stay myself to my nerve's taut, fraught with a virgin's trembling, if for the sake to swindle the brain into mistaking she held the shadow of a wind. That I walked the ghostly streets, incited to flee those essences or become them, whose voices gather and spin the brain in rallying to blow the top, myself and the offended shadows of coyotes, and begging whatever justice there might be that has delivered me up the last that I might stumble into fulfillment of that which has goaded me out, that I should take his tremulous throat right there and surrender him to the ground and in doing catch the final whisper like a butterfly in a net who by his fluttering can jam the pistons that work the need deepdown, to leave him as he fell, splayed amid plain sight, the bodied signature of my passing.

I sneak out the back. The day is aflame with clouds and hurts my eyes, even when they have grown used to it.

As I walk past, people tip their hats. Sunday ladies bow reluctant, for they can scent my trade is death. To them I am not so much a man as a power they must solicit, a thing that may or may not acknowledge their bedtime prayers, the way skin may or may not grow back depending on the depth of the wound or the way a wished-for rain may scourge the roots. I am that governance they hope protects them and yet that stands outside the wheel, an idea that moves beyond questions, since their staying afraid gives them the excuse to stay so paltry.

Almost at my fence, having planned to spend the afternoon fishing in the manner of my uncle enjoying a Sunday on the wharf, I find George and Francis McGriff waiting for me on my porch. Then there is Sid, who is leaning against a post and playing knucklebone. For a second the blood reins in my veins. Hesitates, then flows in reverse. The liquid crashing back where I stand, the impact it generates stunning the arteries, crashing against the heart. They look at me as if my presence were something objectionable, as though they preferred a hallucination, a heathen, a cannibal, anything other than what they are forced to contend with now.

"You know you could have gone in," I smile, "instead of sitting out on the porch." I say this in order to sound agreeable, but also to offer the dare.

"True. But I'd hate to be shot dead for a robbery I meant as a neighborly visit," says Francis.

"What can I do you boys for this morning? I don't recall ever inviting you over for dinner?"

"Where you been all morning, Les?" says Francis. "But then we ain't checked round any altars. You figure we should've checked there?"

"Figured I'd do a speck of camping. I couldn't sleep last night and wandered up the ridge. Why, what's all the fuss?"

"Safe's been robbed again," says Sid.

"Only this round we done got them."

"Well," George says, "got one of them anyways." His face is sleep-deprived and he looks dead in spite of himself.

Upon opening the door to the bank, the magic odor of Death comes close to bringing me off my heels, so steeped in the air it is. Had I truly understood this would happen, I would have spread my sleeping quilt next to George; I would have been the one to work this business.

He leads us to the outer safe where, to my sheer surprise, a sight that remonstrates my conscience awaits: I am eaten up with envy that this is pure George, that this is George's handiwork. And thereupon he proceeds to tell just how it came about, how he heard the shouts of the fellow caught in the grip of the trap and rushed in on them, how then there was firing—we study the marks of the bullets on the safe, the chips in the marble walls—at the minimum there were three of them, he explains—and how resigning himself that he was being ushered to Death's doorstep was miraculously startled when they ceased without warning and turned on themselves, shooting the trapped one where he stood and thence made their escape.

"They knock you down on their way out?"

"Nope," says George. "There."

"Come looky here, Les."

We skirt the silent carcass. McGriff shoulders forth the door, which allows a dim light to enter, enough to adumbrate a hole where there once had been floor.

"I told you I ain't lent no keys," says McGriff. I am speechless. "Pretty damn something?"

"That's a mighty big rat hole," says Sid.

"Any you boys been down?"

The silence admits otherwise.

I can smell a faint, dark breeze drifting from somewhere deep in the gap's internals, which runs into my brain, earthy and ancient, real. From whence did this wind originate? They are the sighs of the damned slogging away at their punishment.

"By all means feel free to take a peak. You just have yourself a nice little stroll, pack you a pleasant picnic. Hell, this might be a brand-new beginning for me, the recreation business. Only I can't much promise they ain't down there waiting around the corner, itching to club you a good one or shoot your nose right off. Least that's why George here's afraid of the dark."

McGriff chuckles and George grunts.

"You can tell how they broke out," says Sid's voice.

He shows us the scratch marks around the lockwork. Childish astonishment is all I can think to reveal.

After a while my tongue is able to figure the words, though it is not Sheriff Les who is saying them, nor is it the one behind—nothing except a lesser breeze runneling off a major wind.

"George, you deserve a medal for this. That or a mighty big raise. Either way, there's gonna be a prize coming your way. We'll publish this in the paper."

"Thank you, Leslie."

I move beyond them and squat down next to the corpse. "So this is the fellow whose partners rathered him shot than unfix his foot." Savoring the false moment, which would have hung within my reach had I just stayed, though I insist on pretending it may still, for the instant I no longer do it will no longer feel so valid, all of them, but another of those misfires that I must admit was not quite right.

I touch the familiar dungarees, rotten, excoriate, pants that only a dead man can make look good. I release the pin of the trap, but the teeth are stuck against the bone, and it takes all the strength I can muster to draw it from the skin. I kick the trap from the body.

"Sure you don't want this bear for a handsome rug?" says Francis.

Now, having deferred the instant long enough, I turn him over and feast my sight upon his portrait. He is dead, no getting round it. No hope of a last cache of breath. I can tell where each of the five shots has entered the skull: the bone, blood, and flesh in magnificent corollas curled from tissue, waves of shocked, burnt skin. He has neither lips nor cheeks nor nose, a small gobbet for part of an eyeball. The thick hair of curls give a stark juxtaposition to the ghastly face below, if a face you can call it.

I imagine this man coming toward me on the street to ask my offhand advice and that horrible horrendous portrait forcing me to run, the sight mortifying my soul.

"Handsome some bitch, ain't he?" says Francis. "What I don't get is why he'd want to shoot down his own partner over again that way. Why not once, put the bastard out of his misery if he didn't want us to hang him, catch him and squeal on them other boys? It just don't make much good sense to shoot him again and again like that."

I bend down closer; I can smell the stale sweat on him still clouding his skin, the particular musk that is his smell: an odor of horses, clay, powder, urine.

Though I have observed thousands of corpses, something about this one with its lank and twisted leg that lies stiff as corpses and continues to stay dead nevertheless suggests volition, that he is choosing to stay in that attitude, and should I offer him a hefty thump on the back after wiping the grease from his mouth he would yet linger still and dead—my blow working through his chest and bowels—and then would slowly twitch with life to no one's great surprise.

I rifle his pockets, careful about what I may find, but barring a pipe and tobacco pouch, which evinces a penchant for burley, a few spare caps, a photograph of a nude woman and stallion, he has nothing identifying that might be used to sift a name.

"You want me to go round up the buggy and we can bury him?" says George. "I'm about ready to sleep a million years."

Then I catch from him a look. In his having been kept awake all night and his surprise he has found the dawn, in that somber stern gaze of his he wears day over day, another look slinks at the bottom, on the floor of a remonstrative abyss: he is accusing me face to face. Through the weird prism of his eyes not only can I trace the reflection of my jealousy, that I desperately wish I had been here—though he did not shoot the body, it is almost as if he had, since had he not burst in they would not have panicked among themselves (in his unaffected swagger, George boldly declaims with a taunting sweep of the arm that he has pilfered his last breath, has listened to the boy expire among the gunshots and resounding echoes, the breath's final spill let go and skittering among the smoke for only a true specialist to distinguish, detect, to savor)—but I gather he thinks I *was* here. In the common instant we share a look, plummeting to the floor where his worst suspicions fester and breed their egregious monsters that cannot be killed once born. And it is there I lie squinting up at him, the distant light besmeared by abstruse murk. I read that in fact George thoroughly hates me, despises me, every layer of his being desiring my painful torture, and from there I read his theory that has become his private law: that indeed I was here last night robbing the bank and shooting at him (I myself in the dark confidence aimed my pistol into the dead boy's skull and fired his brain four times—I did this for hating George), that in fact he and McGriff have been scouring the vault all morning for some clue of my association, and only after casting forth their hopes did they determine to lead me in for the sole purpose of studying me, my reaction, for some gesticulative evidence in lieu of finding my badge planted by the corpse, a clue, a sign, an admission. I know they both want me dead, and now I can feel the dark wind welling, rising toward me and beginning to come; I can feel the wind that cannot be stopped.

The three of them are watching me closely. In their studying me they offer a judgment at once keen and strange, a look that says I am the bad idea they cannot help thinking, and they are waiting for that hideous matter to crawl forth out of my throat and plap down on the floor, a mucus-rid creature hacked up for their dissection.

"You said there were others. How many others were there?"

"Least two or three," says George. "Maybe a good passel more."

"Like to they fled town. Made off with what they grabbed on the first round. Least that's what I'd do. If they was smart they'll never ride within a hundred miles of here again in their life. Well, at least they left half their money I can stave off them Highland Row folks with. In the meantime I got to plug this damn hole up and pay some fella to hike out to where that cave leads in so every Robinson Crusoe ain't lining up, taking turns busting through my safe."

"I believe we saw the last of them boys," says George, his voice a dreary hope.

Now I can feel it cooling against my skin (it steams not from George nor Sid nor from any leak in the cave but from a pinpoint in the future, seconds as fleet as lightning on a day I know not when, but there inevitable as sleep): it tells me I must, I will, have got to now, for the question is ultimately choiceless, and should I dare to think to fight it or attempt to ignore the call, every moment from now on in between will bear the accruing weight of tremulous disobedience, no choice but to move forward and abet, assisting it how I can, lest the deed turn against the doer, the handiwork strike the hand, or the night take action and blear the stars.

"The gold was stacked to here?"

"Yonder a bit," says Sid. "Yeah, there."

"Enough to press a stout horse to death," says McGriff.

"I think they're still in the neighborhood," I say.

Blank blinking faces: canvasses awaiting the paint of my thoughts.

"And how come you think that, Sheriff?"

"Gold the amount they stole is an investment of more than aplomb. It's an investment mainly of time. I'm talking days, maybe even weeks, to move it all. That is, if we're in agreement they'd want to store it and spend it far away from the place they stole it from, and you said yourself there were two left at bare minimum."

"Maybe," says George. "Probably a couple more."

"Maybe they got a team working for them whose chore it is working to tote it all. Running it off in cycles. But then think about it: Would *you* do that? I'd prefer keeping the shares as scant as possible."

And indeed they start to think. I begin before they can think too hard.

"You see, I think they're still pretty close, and I'd be quick to go and speculate that there's even a good chance we can nab the rest of them boys. Especially if we got good bait."

"And what good bait would that be, Sheriff? Assuredly you ain't talking about no more of my gold."

"The bait would be that body."

Each of their brains is crisscrossed now, and I am unable to make out whether they abhor my words or happily agree on account of the breeze I can tell is coming, that trickle of dark wind.

"Les, what do you have in mind?" says George.

"What I have in mind is we take that felon's corpse, hang it up on our gate, and don't let no folks take it down that ain't his partners in crime. Strange folks that come prowling around, inquiring about what's the big old deal or raising a ruckus, we note them and we watch them."

"Hell, Les," says Francis, "if it were me I'd just as soon leave him up there to rot. Ain't no way I'd go risking my neck just to get a dead body into the ground. You'd have to have less marbles than I give them credit."

"I don't think the revival folks'll go for that business no more," says George. "This ain't the same frontier it used to be."

The body sprawled at our feet waits in such a manner you would think it seems to agree, is begging to be hoisted up on the gate, where he can enjoy a view of the town and, like a proud flag hectoring the enemy, simply by a look, espouse defiance.

"Look," I say, "you can blame the whole thing on me, tell whatever big rap it brings that it was all my idea and mine alone. And very likely it *will* do nothing but sit up there and stink and putrefy in the sun, in which case I'll be happy to go up and lug it down myself. But, gentlemen, please. If they really are still with us, as I very much suspect, then seeing their partner strung up on the gate will at least serve to rile their feathers. Fan more smoke to fire their hornets' nest. And my guess is we'll see some sign soon enough, a sign to show they've been hiding here amongst us the whole time, and by golly they won't be happy. Because when you ain't much thinking straight it's all the easier for you to go on and get yourself caught. So what do you boys say?"

13

He took Irving's horse along with the mule, though it quickly became apparent that the mule was holding them back, ignoring any challenge to its laggard walk of preference, an insubordinate, slow gait by which it could plod and sleep at once. Having cursed the animal and thrashed it, threatening to shoot the beast and leave the carcass for carrion in the plains, finally in enraged exasperation he halted them, from the mule taking his scant chattels and wishing it a gentle if bitter farewell, and left it to the hope of someone's chancing. Indifferent, the mule stood where he'd left it and watched him go.

After a moment of riding alone, he cast back, a slight concern for the old beast's fate, but in the vast expanse of plain he saw nothing except land and a dim premorning hint in the east. He wondered if he had left it where he thought or if the mule had died precisely on his quitting or if that lucky stranger had already chanced past and gone.

An extinct sunrise bloomed from an ashen dawn spawning colors like the charred remains of rich-hued flowers, which choked the sky with unclean whites and grays. To steel himself from going mad when the events of the night came rushing back, he tried consoling himself by quoting axioms about the nature of things and transience, heedful that everything if it were not yet so would soon become the stuff of cinders, life and deeds and conflicts, like last millennium's wars, merely whispering sands in an hourglass.

For much of the day he saw no one. Not a house, fence, or farm. All lay quiet—hearing the breeze and patterned hooves and jostling baggage until that too became part of the quiet—a mute reality to the hills as if the landscape itself, frightened by his intrusion, were feigning a defensive death, and he dared not venture off his saddle for fear he startle it.

A few times a day he passed lone men or parties that, jogging on the edge of the horizon in a way that seemed they were straining not to fall off, inanimate shapes shimmering to life in the veiled air, a tedious, eventual growing yet a staid hovering all the same, after long anticipation, passed swiftly by his side—mute, dreary, anonymous, the half-alive offspring of this phantom territory. As the strangers rode by, he imagined them ambushing and marching him off, their guns aroused in his spine, toward a bend in a creek. Preparing himself to die, knowing it was over and thinking to himself: Yes, this is just, how right this is, for the however many souls I have robbed of returning to their mothers who must have cursed me and begged this death once they found out that I was the torturer who reduced their hopeful faces to scowls, because I cut down what they most loved, and cut it down so wantonly; yes, this is just, how right. Then feeling the swarm of bullets enter him and hack his skull to dust until his brain tampered out in vague acquiescence.

At nights, in the pointed light of the fire, he fondled his three ingots. Revolving them in his fingertips as if to ensure that nothing about them had faded or transfigured, that the day's ride had not rendered them some alloy or his brother's stale blood had not proven the catalyst to permute them from gold to dross. Turning his stretched and warped reflection from one plane to the next.

He was studying Irv's Remington, the weight of it confident and foreign but familiar in his palm. (A while ago he had owned a gun very similar: whereas this was the Navy thirty-six, he had owned the heavier Army, which he had depended on and loved and reluctantly gotten rid of. Over the years he had nurtured the solitary pursuit of testing all kinds of revolvers and living with them for a spell in the same manner that he had heard that skeptical bachelors might court a particular female and examine her in varieties of terms and circumstances through the strain of delayed rewards as if to verify that this were the best right choice, that she will stay true and promised despite whatever threats may occur. He had bought and borrowed dozens of them, and he found the 1858 Remington-Beals Army to be the model of fidelity—he found her aim dependable and accurate, her body staunchly resilient, pristine with subdued beauty, yet no one would single him out just to take it from him, the blued barrel and walnut grip staring back with something of a coquette's kiss farewell—and though he vowed each morning when he set out he would leave the object planted in the fire's cinders, an anonymous metal stump, every evening he had somehow allowed it to stay, which he had not noticed until caught in the trap of looking at it once again, unable to put the thing down, enthralled by its pure stolid beauty, like an old friend whom he appreciated catching up with and liked having on his side regardless of the dangers, the reasons they had parted in the first place.) The closer he got toward home, the more exigent it became as protection, he decided, for he had no clue what to expect.

On the one hand he told himself it was possible that Gruhn and his mother were dead, had died of sickness or age or in an Indian raid or during a winter years ago, that it was probably not even his mother still there in the cabin, if Gruhn's cabin existed at all. Yet on the other he insisted the worst, his memory from those years alone in the fields, the two of them bound in the hard code of toil, delineating the stories his father had entrusted and envisaged for his warning—why he had threatened to shoot him if ever he caught him about, why he insisted he had ruined his wife before they had wed—and it made right sense his uncle would not want him around, would previse his coming and killing him the second he learned it was he.

So he kept Irving's Remington, fighting the wish to use it and assuring himself he would never need to, but not ridding himself of it either lest the need arise.

He passed villages where the accents rang like foreign bells and where children banded together in the silent streets, peering up at him with devouring eyes. He fought the urge to gather them in his saddle and speed them away to safety, to steal them to a peaceable cloister where he could structure their education and ward off the influences that went lurking beyond the schoolyard, a school the best of its kind that he saw as a simple academy for neglected young scholars whom he deliberately selected from the grip of rustic mire while shielding them from the usual regime of hunting, all to be replaced with a reverence for discipline and genuine altruism based on beholding the world as it is, students who, under his tutelage, would wield keen minds that would defend them from having to return to pigpens. But like a shoe that bites the heel of its wearer, the figure of Gruhn kept gnawing at him.

Had Gruhn not intruded and taken what was not his to take and then surrendered it back busted, patched over a thousand times, so that in its long misuse it had become something it was not, Irving would not be dead. Instead he had skewed them all, in particular his brother-in-law's sons, in a deviant undermining as if to retaliate against the sister stolen from him, handing them back to the world endued with the insignia that they belonged now to him like two marked cannonballs he had aimed straight at his enemies, knowing full well that although they would fail to reach their targets, preferring to mow down the unassuming wretches whose only involvement was that Gruhn had gotten them involved, they could not help but entrench themselves miles before hitting their goals, yet through their launching he had worked to summon the original targets closer, to a proximity where Gruhn himself could stick the knife.

It was late one night as he was studying Irving's pistol beside the embers that the thought struck him that he would have to go on and fire it, aware his aim would be pathetic and that if he truly presumed there was any risk he would have to go on and fire it, must practice and get more caps and powder than the amount that was still in the cylinder. First he must rid himself of compunction and understand he was firing it with the right motivation, which was to rescue his mother from the dominion of a horrible man. If he was going to fire it, then it was fitting he get over the nagging of snapping the trigger so that in the future he might focus on sighting the bullet.

With reluctance he took Irving's Remington, cocked it, and aimed it aslant at the stars. His breath picking up as if he had come home to the arms of a woman after forgetting her touch these months. Then it fired. A thunder enraged at the night, subordinating all noise else to deference.

He felt his entire self come alive, the explosion having quickened across his skin. His mind sparkled in attention, and it took him some while that night to fall asleep.

That noon he rode into Shoal Creek and the sense of panic that had been dogging him at last caught up.

People he did not recognize stared at him and scrutinized his strangeness. He lowered his hat. Glancing at windows, doors, and paths for sign of Gruhn.

He considered enlisting the help of the sheriff, of demanding he know their whereabouts and admitting the stories that had poisoned his innocence as proof for rallying to bring him in, but on considering it end to end the actual consequence began to register that, if anything, the slow methodical bureaucracy inherent to the law's paper justice would allow Gruhn the chance to slink between the stamps and signatures to where, having evidence of his nephew's intentions, he would end him among the secrecy. So he knew he could enlist the help of no one but Irving's pistol.

As he recalled the turns in the trail from town to cabin, people waved at him or tipped him hello, each of their movements seeming wrought with insidious danger. He wondered if he had always felt so, anxious approaching fearful, whenever he had traveled through town. Even the trees seemed to lean from the road, waiting to uproot, attack.

It did not take long and then the town was cast behind him. Finding the familiar childhood hills, their bright-etched contours having been engrained in his memory this whole time like the tenor of his voice. Surprised to find the scenery surge to life from a death it had never died, a sudden rushing relief at finding himself in the thought:

Yes, today would make a fine day to die—while groping at new possibilities, at some gentleman's agreement in which he might resign himself to adapting the sordid tales he had heard scarred upon the man until they had covered him a monster of nightmares, at which point he understood that any scant hope of peace or compromise lay as unattainable as a cloud from yesterday's welkin, and to accommodate Gruhn by even a half inch would demand he become someone he was not because it made him an espouser of and thereby a willing participant in those same flagitious wrongs, which only verified it must end for one or both of them today.

He watched the cabin come up in the dale. Trees had been felled that he was certain had once staked the property. Canvasses of wheat skimming in the wind and dimpling with multiple schools of shadows that throbbed in and out. No smoke from the slender chimney.

In his nub he clutched the reins. With his hand he took out the Remington, cocked it by raking his elbow across the hammer, and held it at half aim. If he saw him he was going to shoot him, had better shoot him (though he had bought four spare cylinders and preloaded each, by the time he could effectively hope to reload it he figured he'd be dead).

He tethered his horse at a quiet distance. Encouraging himself. He had the help of surprise: he would walk in, shoot him, exit—if he could manage getting inside without getting shot from here to the door.

Apart from the violent scream of a blue jay he heard nothing, no human noise. Every second expecting a bullet to come slinging through his skull and the world to fall off empty . . . but before I should comprehend its doing so.

There were bootprints preserved in clay, equal to his own. At a glance the farm seemed tended, and he could see how they might have left and moved across the country or perhaps died years ago.

He crept up, clenched for anything that might of a sudden erupt. Treading as if on a thunderhead. His hearing narrowed to sift any noise, he waited, pressed against the wall. On the periphery he sought any object that might be attempting to hide from or sight him as he listened for some sharp noise, for some intention around the door. He felt the whole day watching him, readying.

Finally when he could stand the quiet no longer, having heard no volatile sign, no betrayal of animation stir from around the corner, intuiting that with the longer he lingered outside there occurred the compounding likelihood of Gruhn arriving and sighting him, he resolved to venture indoors.

The door was open. Slowly he let himself in. He saw the room contained sparse furniture, the fetor ancient, intimate, vulnerable. He perceived a stove, a table and four chairs, a chest, a bed, and he watched a phantom tableaux of them huddled together in winter, the thousands of meals he had missed now burgeoning over the table and that rare wisp of conjecture, an aside fallen between crumbs, wondering what if anything had become of him, and wishing he had been their age that he might have been able to share things from the old days, and so powerfully did this fancy captivate him he did not behold in front of him the short frail woman staid like an object in the room.

Though she had not moved, he cried out, spooked. She was already turned toward him, but now she leaned in stiffly, a dead door on its hinge.

"Mother!" he cried aloud.

He watched her, fearing even a blink should give her cause to disappear. In a dizzy of seconds he tried to exhume what this senescent figure had been to him, to find the fruit immured in the pit. He ventured a step forward.

"No," he heard a thin voice creak, a shy imperative. He stopped.

"No?"

"No, but I knew you'd to. Ain't no use in worrying when I reckon you'll get rid of me howmsoever you like, just like them other ones done before you, and I'll bear it on out the same."

Beyond the door the noon light was swollen painful; he saw she was fumbling with the strings of her bonnet.

"Here," he said, "I'll do it."

Softly he approached, sure to smile, until they two were nearly touching noses. She let him tie the strings in a bow.

She looked like a person he used to know, someone whom Life had stuck a syringe in and drawn to the point where one drop more and she would be dry as dust. She stared at him, but not looking.

"Do you know me, Mother?" he whispered somehow serenely. "It's me, Edward. Your eldest son."

Her head twitched; she seemed to recognize the familiar sounds, yet their substance eluded her grasp.

"Edward." She said this almost tasting it.

"Yes," he said, "that's right."

She squinted past him for a long time, perhaps suggesting that she was trying to behold something that was not there, perhaps remembering him but smaller, perhaps, the compartments of memory having withered and cracked with the age, in jogging the contents to mind it meant fixing a faded image to an even more futile frame. Then the blood coursing through her must have quickened, since her stare caught a spark of that old fire, and she nodded, his dark picture in her eyes waked to life.

"Edward!" she cried, and fell against him as if the weight of saying his name were too much to let go.

"Oh Mother!"

He held her. A frail sack of bones ready to slip loose of their tendons. Not dissimilar from cradling air. Part of him wanting to run and part of him wanting to stay to confirm that this was real. An enormous tenderness shrouded his heart.

"Edward, why has it taken you so long coming home? We thought you dead these years."

"I know, mother, I'm sorry. I should have sent you word, I know. I know I should have and I didn't." Searching his choked lexicon that he might render the notions logical. He held her in his arms, continued to insist her beyond mere acquaintance.

"You come here to tell me something, Eddie. That's why you come home."

"Yes," he said, on the verge of bawling.

"They's a body to put in the ground."

"Yes."

"Who's it that's dead?"

"It's Irving, Mother. Irving's dead."

"Who?"

"Irving, your son. He died about a week ago. I'm sorry I have to tell you."

Sad she seemed but stoic, and he wondered if she knew she was not all right, all there, if by giving him few words she realized he would have to appraise them beyond their value, reading in them more than there lay to pick up, as if their catch had eluded his grasp and that failure was on account of his own clumsiness. She had the air of an angel's sloughed skin.

"The war?"

"No," he answered. "I'm sorry to have to be the one to tell you."

"Did they bury him, Irving?"

"I couldn't say. Maybe, but I don't think."

"We'll have to see to it. I didn't figure his for the one that's been vexing me, but I been known to be mistook."

Scattered old woman tossing on Death's river. Reaching out and linking fingers, only to be bobbed back whirling amongst the current. Would my staying have kept you from plunging in?

Then he saw the bed—had seen it in the corner all the while—in the dammed light, under a window begrimed with filth, though now that he truly perceived it his nerves pricked up again.

"Where's Uncle Gruhn?" he asked, his voice bordering on demand.

Motes in the room drifting a dreamy hurry, it took her some searching before she found whatever she'd been seeking.

"Gruhn," said her cracked voice. "Gruhn went out on business. He should be back any day. I can tell him you stopped in."

Fighting pictures he did not wish to reflect on, he felt at this instant he had to kill something or he himself would be killed. He wanted to ask her, to shout in her face: Has Gruhn done this? What has he done? Tell me everything!

Then once I hear hand me the gun to blow out my brains along with the deeds, to eradicate them at the origin.

"I'll fix coffee."

He caught her wrist, and recognizing his alarm, she seemed to understand what he meant. She let him stay her.

"Gruhn's coming home. If he ain't buried he ain't kept down. Promise me, Eddie. Promise."

"Yes, Mother. I promise. Only we have to hurry. I'm going to bring you far away from here and we can't ever come back. Ever."

Two to the saddle, returning the way he had come. A vast pall to the sky that unscrewed time from the heavens, the sun nothing to null.

Often as they sped he would start without warning—that feeling of plummeting just as you fall asleep—and missing her clinging would cast back behind him, expecting to find her tossed off: nobody save the space from which he was fleeing. But there she was, always behind, her light wasted husk barely a casket of life on the cantle and softly holding to him, herself a tender breeze. She slept like that all the night.

14

Not until they had been married eight years did he take fire at Gruhn.

It happened that something told him to leave the fields sooner than usual. The sky breaking up and remending itself so that all looked as it was. And returning to the house, his suspicions were confirmed: for there out in the open, as unbecoming a sight as if they were desperately hidden, he found his wife fallen in Gruhn's arms.

He was holding her against his chest in a gesture that declared it would not be long until they could steal away to some foreign land where they could forget the troubles that had worked to keep them apart.

As for his wife, he could not make out her face, though by her stance he gathered she'd acquiesced since the beginning, that or Gruhn had forced her to and she had learned to all the same.

"Hidy, Gruhn!" called Les. "What we got here underway?"

From his vantage he watched the two of them start and sunder. It was not immediate; in fact, it appeared to take them a great effort to begin to force themselves apart, such as knit stems that are disentangled and yet continue to bend toward how they grew.

As if to behold that he were real, he could feel his wife's eyes seek him before darting back to the ground. From his vantage she appeared less a woman than an image in a pool that a raindrop or breeze comes ruffling over or dispels to something inadequate, lost, her slouch conveying that she expected at any instant that hungback drop to come.

Brother and sister waited. In the attending silence he heard the curses they wanted to scream, recognizing in that terrible quiet the same most intimate noises they had forged before he had startled them, which they now turned and aimed on him with ironic effortlessness. Gruhn held an arm propping up his wife.

"Tell me, Les," called Gruhn. "Why is it every time I come by and see my sister, I find more and more marks up on her? Ain't no fool so clumsy he falls as much as she."

The sun beat in and out. At one second it was noon; at the next it could have been dusk. Then without looking at either, her gaze in mournful communion with the ground or in the manner of somnambulists who will stare and stare at nothing, the woman said, her voice scarcely a whisper:

"I done it. Picked them up by accident when I was helping Les patch stalls. Guess I didn't mean to."

Though Gruhn kept as he was, you could tell a drift of surprise had parted his grimace, his aspect that of seeking the air and trying to sift how Les had done it, made her to utter those words by devious telepathy.

"You don't mean to do a lot of things, and yet somehow you manage to mean. Kind of like how I mean to put a stop to this right now."

"Hold it, Gruhn."

"Leslie, Annora might be your wife, but first she was my sister. And there might be no law saying a man can't lay a hand against his wife, but so long as I'm around it's as well there ain't."

"I know there's a law against rape."

At that the sun pulsed out. It was as if in saying it he had somehow killed the day. Neither of them wished they possessed the strength to continue from where they had been led, and yet turning back was impossible.

It came out almost a clearing the throat of phlegm.

"What rape?" said Gruhn.

The sun throbbed back with the heat of revelation; the air turned thin and bright.

"Not a, Gruhn: multiple. Deliberate violations of the law and nature."

Gruhn swallowed. He was staring hard at something. Whether a memory he hoped to have gotten rid of that now truncated his sight or the world as it lay in pieces, which he was trying to fit back together, recall how it once had been. Trembling, she rested against his arm.

"You've lost your goddamn mind, Leslie. You ain't got no proof."

"How about the proof of my wife as witness. One word from her and you'll be screwing the noose, old boy. You'll make a fine offering for some mighty appreciating flies."

"You always got exaggerated notions about things you don't know nothing about. Your head's a muddled mess."

"I've got the law to sort that for me. And next time I catch you here I'm gonna prosecute you till you're a handsome blue in the face. At least Simon's learned not to cross my fence. You come between a man and his wife and there'll be awful hell to pay. I can swear to that."

The day yet harsh and blinding, it was Gruhn that dampened now as a part of him changed directions. He took the brace of his arm from his sister, who fell back sharply, then at the last instant was caught by some invisible prop, and ignoring Les, he turned to her, his aspect a different man's.

"Just go see him, Ann—if you can. He doesn't have much time."

Without touching her or bidding farewell, he marched off down the plain, his good leg leading like a laborious priapus, back to his cabin a half mile yonder on land he had refused to concede to Les in spite of that Les had offered him a sum threefold its value.

His presence continued. Even when he was gone from sight and night had come, the words and man continued seething in his chest like the dark burning of the stovelight, and in that stovelight he plied her for the intimates, but she refused to bare even the slenderest account of what had passed between them or between them and others, would admit neither coercion nor brute malignity nor curious acquiescence, and so he hit her across the chin using the back of his hand, hoping it would serve the midwife to the particulars he feared but needed to hear.

When she insisted on raving, he hoped by hitting her again it would sharpen her muddled tongue. The struck sides of her face where the marks had blossomed looked the rouge suggestions of a slattern.

"He didn't do. Didn't do, didn't. He came to tell me bout Pa."

"'Tell me, tell me'—what about Pa? Then why were you letting him touch you after all you've said and done? I walked up and there you were like Romeo and Juliet. Explain to me that if you dare."

Her underlip quivering, afraid to say the wrong answer.

"I don't know" was all she said.

He hit her again. A blow that spun her backward in a whirling dance that would have been graceful had she not ended crashing into the table.

Once she recovered she said, "Please stop hitting me."

"I don't want to, Ann. Just tell me how come you told me those things and now say they didn't happen? That or can't or won't or don't remember. That doesn't make any sense."

She, having crouched under the table in trust it might swallow her in disguise, fell on herself, cowering.

"I don't know."

"You don't know *what*!"

"Don't know, don't know, don't know. Oh God!"

He sighed, the blood in his fingers from the shocks going softly vibratory as if they formed a stranger's hand.

"I didn't mean for it to happen this way," said Les. He spoke calmly. "It's just that—you're the only one that can rile me up this way, going on and saying his name. Then you say nothing happened. I promise you once I know for sure I'll never do this again, I swear. Then I can be solid knowing how the bastard lays."

On the other side of the wall Edward held the twins, who were crying and wanting to go to her.

"This is all Gruhn's fault," he told them. "Gruhn is at the root of this."

The next morning he was gone. They found his bed empty and no sign of him outside. Not in the barn or in the fields. They found he had taken his horse.

As a gray sun tunneled over plains stooped with dew, they decided to take on his chores since they dreaded more his upset if they did not than his anger at doing them wrong.

Racing from one task to the next, they were to finish his chores before turning to their own. They brought the horses to the paddock, and prior to that they cleaned their hooves. They freshed the stalls and carried water and filled the woodbox to Les's notch. An emerging lightness intrinsic to a festival day. Annora and Irv against Eddie and Quinn. Not that they did not still absolutely fear him, but it soon became apparent he really was not there, not just out of sight: he had vanished entire! His presence sunk to a voice, a loud echo igniting their work and fanning them to hurry, who bent their thoughts to constant attentive care to ensure they were exacting his rigorous standards of futility, but those standards soon constituting the very rules for the games they were rushing to win. Whether a competition as to who could carry the most fodder without spilling or come out first of a row after checking the nubbins for rot, all rendered a sort of game, a reason to hurry and finish, an enactment of his gestures transformed into a happy if blasphemous pageant, the theme of which became the ridiculous confession of how fiercely each of them had watched him throughout the years. Which quickly did escalate. Hurrying in Les's lanky gait, in Les's stiff akimbo. A Les that waddled like a constipated duck. Who then became a blind duck. Who then offered his outsized wings that threatened to topple him, who then did topple.

By late morning they had finished. Light-headed from racing and laughing, they did not know if he was ever returning. (He had never just left like that, had never woke without setting upon his chores, without probing for infractions and ways of preventing those that might creep in, his vigilance evoking the code of a lone warrior determined to please his lord, for even the days it rained he seemed to study the dreary weather, not to be disturbed, as though calculating its strategy or comparing its martial theory yet searching for some point of failure by which he might persevere.) And it was this fierce discipline that they continued to mock and stage when they returned to work after breakfast.

At once they heard the jogging of his horse. They saw Les bumping up on his mare.

Though the sky had been overcast, something about the day went dark, the air thin and sterile as it must be in thawless tundra.

They saw he was nursing a bulge on his shirt, which he kept fighting to hold still.

"Why are you out here working?" he told them from his saddle. "Today is supposed to be a holiday."

"What's that?"

"What's that moving on your belly, Pa?"

"What? You must mean this." And fishing it forth from his stomach, he produced for them a bright black dog—a blinking puppy who vacillated between worship for its carrier and yearning for the strangers below.

"Is he for me?" screamed Quinn.

"Can I pet him, Pa?" said Irving.

"No, I saw him first! I get to pet him!"

Les fought his horse, which was attempting to turn him around. He called down on them, "The dog is not for either of you. It's a special present for an acquaintance that we are going to go visit today. Help me hitch the wagon."

"Yes, sir," said Edward.

"Pa," said Irving once he saw him eye to eye, "can I . . . I want to hold him. Can I, sir?"

"No." He spoke the word like the chop of a knife. "Only I am getting to hold him. He's a special present for Simon, and only Simon is getting to hold him. Is that understood?"

But already their faces had ripened with tears. Which caused the puppy to clamor, and it fought Les's grip in an attempt to leap off the horse, into their arms.

Even after they braced the team and were some miles out, they continued crying, no matter how much Les promised he'd switch them and heap on the punishments, spates of tears that, whenever the little thing would peak back its head and yap in dismay, burst themselves anew.

In the manner of Les, Edward feigned ignoring them. He watched a hawk overhead go drifting like a message at sea. He wondered about the places the hawk had seen, how and if it remembered them all, if as a dumb beast it held any sense of the past, the mother and siblings whom it had known as a fledgling, or if a bird's memory were as free as it appeared. He thought he should be terrified to persist at such heights beyond the voice of the world, where it was only yourself to keep yourself afloat, and being but a reasonless creature you could not even count on thought for help to flap your wings and suspend you but on the instinct you did not even know you had. With his eyes tracing the lines, he perceived a series of linking Os.

It took a few hours for them to reach Beckenham, where Annora's father had lived from the day he moved there with wife, son, and daughter. He and a small group of thinkers had come west to establish a simple township, the laws that anchored it meant to reinstate the values of the Anglo-Saxon destiny, each an earl to his home. They had built each other's estates and ploughed each other's fields, and often they had gathered to practice the ancient tongue and would mourn their losses whenever Death made His frequent rounds.

That first year his own wife had died during a blizzard.

Upon waking from a nap and needing her aid, he rose and drifted to the bed and discovered she had passed without disruption. The way her head leaned on the pillow and her mouth gaped at him suggested she might return at any moment.

Mutely he went and peered through the ice-lacquered pane. Everywhere snow impearled the fields; the world had become a frozen void, the earth too cold to welcome the stabs of a shovel.

He waited until the twins were fast asleep. Then he took her up, gathering his oldest rope, and left to confront the snow.

He trudged beyond his fields. Too cold to mourn, too cold to think. His brain sorely ached and then seemed empty. In that manner he walked several miles.

Again and again, having held the body so long his arms not only went numb and it seemed she hung before him suspended, hovering before him by trick, but her corpse was beginning to bow, the length of her curling as if to shield him from the razorous winds and lend him what final warmth she possessed, as if even in death she were proving her better love that continued to vex and chide him for his cruelty in leading her hence from her family of pedigree and that was now offering her temple to the elements, he dropped her into the snow. After fishing around a spell, fearing he would never be able to locate her until the extinction of history, was relieved to strike a part—a leg, a bit of waist, a nose—and hefted her up, emerging from the depths an erased figure to bear her through the ice.

When finally he reached the glade, his head was spinning and he doubted his fingers would work his will. Using his wrists and teeth, he managed to tie the knot, hurled it across the sturdiest-looking branch of a nodose, snow-covered beech tree. Up he raised her, strove, her spindly feet dangling just beyond his stretch, not quite the height from which she had deigned to judge yet high enough to outlast the season, and he sped back through the pale dark, his mouth too chittering to upbraid the frostbite that was abusing his being to the soul, back to the warmth of his home.

The next day his children inquired what had become of her. He told them, "God has taken her," and they seemed content sorting this out.

That spring, once the last heaps of snow had finished leaking and the dirt could withstand the stick of a thumb, he resolved that it was time.

He was not a drinking man, but asking his Maker's forgiveness, he bought the cheapest bottle of brandy and downed as much of it as he could stand. Then, taking a blouse that had been his wife's and recalling he needed the shovel, he trudged back to where he'd hanged her.

A nervous haste to his rapid though muddled steps. The burgeoning land, its millions of tiny green tongues, a chorus thrashing at him and chiding: he had already waited too long; he had wasted the best of the season; he must hurry and set to working his fields.

A good ways yonder he tied her blouse around his nose, figuring an unbecoming bandit of strange compulsions, and preparing himself to be frightened, he crept into the glade.

Since he had last seen it, the glade had flowered with the chatter of sparrows and the odor of earth in thaw. Petite leaves sheltered their branches like embarrassed matrons' fingers covering their nudity. But when he got to the beech tree, no rope or wife hung waiting for him. It was as though she had tired of waiting.

He stared up blankly at the tree. In his staring the primal desire that he might render the job done without lifting a finger. Neither was she higher than he remembered nor lower, nor had she skipped to another branch nearby.

He knew that he was drunk, yet not so drunk to claim he had missed the tree and not so addled to ignore the certain gushing of his wife's fire, that welter as had bellowed by the scandal of the minister having been caught stark naked in the chancel with three upright young choristers or had fed on the unfortunate occasion when he had forgotten Annora at the fair, returning home instead with a carved nose whistle and a sack of popped corn under his arm, thinking he had done well for himself, her remonstrative shrill making plain his faulty list of idiocies—her death, the day of her death, her trapped inside months of freezing, for not burying his solemnly sworn wife but stringing her up like an inn sign or flag of a heathen country—scourging him to his knees in an attempt to find some remnant, some clue, some crude assuagement, if only a meager knucklebone, something he might commit to hopeful ground that should cast out the terrible fussing, make her hush and still.

Long past what felt an entire day spent in desperate confusion, his trousers stained with proof he had tried and come up wanting, as he peered into the stream (the slight thought nudging him he should drown himself if only to offer amends), not at his unsorted visage but at the water he lapped down his throat, in the shadows of the setting sun, there in the depths he spotted it: his rope. Curled up and reclining against the silt like a coiled snake he dared not rouse, it had the look of a thing she had done herself. One of those chores he had always planned on finishing but kept forgetting about getting round to that she had finally gone and managed herself, having wearied of his excuse.

So she had buried herself. To his relief she had gotten her aim. He agreed his job was done.

They reached the crossing place for Beckenham, their stomachs in dialogue. Under the spell of the afternoon Annora had slept for much of the journey as had the puppy, which Les was cradling to his chest while with his right hand he worked the reins. Its little legs dangling over his palm swayed and wavered to the rhythm of the wagon.

He lived about a mile east of the village, and turning on the tracks to his home, they saw him sat amid a field, his company a lusk cow, himself bereft of a shirt and his squat chest sagging like the breasts of a nursing ape.

On coming near they saw he was rummaging a fallow field in quest of four-leaf clovers and humming a tune of a single note. At first he failed to sight them until one of the horses blew. Startled, he glared back over his shoulder as if interrupted in important business, yet his manner wafted to joy when he noticed they'd brought horses.

"Hello!" he sang, exalting.

They lifted a travelweary hello.

"Tie the horses and water them."

"Do you want me to use his fodder?"

"If he has some, use it."

Les, leveling it before his gaze, stroked the flabby being to life.

"Rise and shine, my little love compan," he whispered, kneading its black skull. "We must shake the blanket of these sleepies."

He did not think to offer them anything, and foraging through the cupboard, she found no trace he had eaten in weeks. She had not been back since before her children were born, and now as she went about two smells vied for her concern: the scent of childhood—of winter fires at odds with snow, dark shadows caressing her knitting, and of the sugar cookies Simon loved, mordant in the wood—against the odor of fleshy decay, the sweet, putrid stink of the body loosening from its fixity.

"What you been eating, Pa?"

"Oh, a little of this, a little of that."

"They any chickens?"

"I don't see why there should be." He said this apparently indignant she should ask.

"Gruhn's been bringing him food," Les called from the other room. "He must be stuffing him full when he can. Doing it every couple of days."

"Who'd you say you were?"

He looked at her, but in his beholding he seemed to be looking at nobody.

"It's me, Pa."

"Say, you must be my wife. Say, this lion's a mighty mean thorn in need of pulling. You up to giving her a tug?"

Edward returned from the stable. He watched the ineffable agony with which the twins were studying the puppy and its attempts to rid itself of Les's grip. It yelped and scrambled, fought to be set down.

"Take them outside," Les told him, his stare sharp like metal. "And keep out until I call."

"Yes, sir," said Edward. "Looks like it's out for us."

Wrangling them through the frame, out into the loom-work of gray cloud. Young voices sank among vast space.

"I'm hungry," said Irving.

"Yeah, when the hell do we eat?"

A wind rose up and took them, and there was silence except for light incessant whining. It was then the old man noticed the dog.

"Say, what you got there?" he ventured, pointing. "That some kind of baby raccoon?"

Les set it down on the ground, and the animal darted for the old man's feet.

"He's for you, Simon. A gift."

Instantly the puppy set about licking the crevices between his toes—his nails were bestial talons—in a bid for some affection. The old man laughed from the pit of his belly as if all the world were so carefree.

"You can pick him up, you know. Just be forewarned he'll nip. That's his way of doting."

Les sat down in the chair. He and Annora watched him confide his tenders, poking and jabbing the creature, these mismatched fondles small tortures meant to be little kind-nesses.

"Yes, sir," the old man cooed. "You're a good raccoon, ain't you, boy. You like that, don't you, raccoon."

Already they were inseparable, the pet the very embodiment of his lithe heart, for he nuzzled it to his breast in the guise of one nursing or hoping he would accomplish it to his own stuff, the two of them even resembling each other like chicks befuddled by their first rain.

Suddenly he peered up, his interest in the puppy made vacuous.

"Who'd you say you were?"

Annora rested against the wall (she would not sit), Les looking on in disgust.

"Who did you think we were?" said Les.

Now the pup was gnawing his beard, fighting the hair in its mouth, and the old man lit up with wonder. This entity conceived for his pleasure. Then backing out, the puppy upturned his head. Each time it peered up at him Simon burst into raucous laughter, simple intenerate joy.

So long had it been Les forgot he had not answered. Then from his delighted oblivion the old man managed to cast out, "I don't know. Just some fella. And my wife's the one over there buttering her bread."

His answer hit like a taunt.

"Simon, why don't you come sit down."

The old man did as told, the puppy falling over itself to be let go. When he set it on the ground it bounded straight for Annora. Having surfeited of her smell, it soon ran to Les to lick his boots. Les gathered the puppy up and began fondling it, just enough so it would not go.

"Who'd you say you were?" the old man muttered.

"Simon, I want to ask you something. I know it's hard to remember, but I need you to try."

"All right."

"Did you and Gruhn . . . did you and Gruhn ever rape Annora, Simon?"

With that the poor woman gasped. As if deflated on herself, she hid in a ball.

"Rape?" The old man spoke, his voice a less certain echo. He smacked a pale lip while he drew the word for an aftertaste, something that might help him comprehend the flavor.

"Rape," he said the word again. "Who raped whom?"

"Annora," said Les. "Right there. And she is not your wife. Annora is your daughter. Tell me why you raped her."

"Well, ain't the gal my wife? Ain't there a certain business goes on between a man and his husband?"

"She is not your wife: she's your daughter, Simon."

"Something wrong these days when a man can't rape his own wife."

"Did you or Gruhn ever rape her, Simon? Was this something you approved?"

In hiding she made not a defensive ball but a ruin, a remnant to a structure whose groundwork has given out.

"I tell you it's the whole durn country's fault. Land's too wide. People too much a number. And those Italians— you know what they are—they get to humping like a den of June rabbits come up to spawn, and before you know it you're part Italian yourself."

"Did you rape Annora, Simon? Did you? Did Gruhn, Simon? Did Gruhn?"

You could see him searching, his narrowed semblance a parody of plumbing a depth, which was actually a skimming of surface.

"Because the sausage fits the bread, and the monkey sneaks to bed."

"I want you to watch this, Simon," said Les. "I have a trick I want to show you."

"All right."

And elevating it before the old man's stare, he took the tiny being that enlivened the moment he set it to ground, only he would not let it go.

"Are you watching me, Simon?" called Les.

"Yes."

And lifting up his bootheel he came down fast upon its skull. An incongruous crunch seemed to stick fast in the room.

"No," she murmured from her huddle.

"Holy hell!" cried the old man, stupefied. "What'd you go and do that for? Why—the baby raccoon, he weren't hurting nobody!"

Forthwith the old man jumped to his feet and commenced a furious pacing of the length of the room. Back and forth he went, muttering nonsense while he rankled his bald crown.

After hardly a minute had gone by he halted near the stove. Having walked himself into dumbness, he appealed to the sense of his onlooker.

"Did I say I was gonna do something?"

"Come and sit down, Simon."

"All right, I think I will."

He dithered there a spell, then some new resolution wafted him back to his seat before the fireplace where he spotted the movements under his boot.

"Say, what you got there under your boot, mister? That look like something to you?" He pointed, almost casual.

"Simon, did Gruhn ever rape Annora?"

"Rape." The old man tasted the word as though he waited to behold the very definition form solid across the air.

"He might of raped Polk's wife yonder ago. Probably raped the whole durn country, Gruhn done. And I tell you what: he's got a lot of rape left in him."

Les removed his bootheel, uncovered the animal merged with the ground. The dead dog's eyes leered up at them, the teeth in a broken grin as if its brains had burst in negotiating a prurient joke.

"Holy hell!" the old man screamed. "What the—what the hell is *that*?" The demented sight a kind of alarm for him to sharpen himself, raise from where he slouched. Tears were slinking down and getting lost in his beard and also forming a glaze over his destroyed face. "Why'd you go do that for?"

"I didn't do that, Simon. You did that."

"*I* did that?"

"What, don't you remember? Shame on you for stomping my puppy. It's not right what you did. Don't you agree?"

But the old man continued to cower. He was fanning away the declaration. Yet for all his revulsion he could not quit looking.

"You did this, Simon. You killed my poor little puppy."

"But why? Why on earth would I do such a thing?"

"Because that's just the way you are."

Again he jumped up and set to pacing the room. Les watched him talk his frantic gibberish while he ruffled the scabs on his head, the path he walked tangled and distracted (perhaps it attested that he hoped to arrive that somewhere physically, however distant it lay in his mind). Again he flagged, then altogether stopped.

"Was I—did I say I was gonna do something?"

"Come sit down, Simon," Les told him.

"Sigh-man. Sigh-man, sit down. A man's got to sit down some day." And he clucked his tongue.

He sat as he had, before the hearth. His posture revealing he was bored but willing to comply, like an eight-year-old in the pews. Soon he noticed the boot.

"Say, you got something on your leg? You step in a mighty big cow pad, mister."

Les withdrew his foot.

"Lord amighty!" the old man belted. "That's a dead dog on the floor! How the hell'd that happen?"

"You did that, Simon."

"*Me?*" he said. "*I* did that?"

"I brought my puppy over to play, but you didn't like him, did you? So when he went sniffing round your pizzle, do you know what you did then? Then you—"

He stomped and stomped it and the whole cabin shook; the dead thing's guts ejaculated a bloody juice.

"Because you're a crazy, child-raping, selfish old man, and the only companion you deserve is a mashed-up puppy on the floor!"

Grabbing Annora, who fought him to remain in her ball, he dragged her from the cabin and summoned his sons. As they prepared to drive home they could hear the old man's yells cleave the air now and then.

A few days later around dusk Gruhn rode up, a punishing gait heard from a distance, but when Les fired at him point blank, aiming to rid himself of him for good, Gruhn pulled to and instantly turned back, and that was the last time Les caught him about.

15

I can tell the dark wind is rising good now. Not from me or from George Cilton, since it is a wind not from any person, though personal it means to come. No wind from any living thing that will find themselves in the ground. It is the wind of an unhealing wound from somewhere across the plain, a crevice in some Delphi. A wound of immense decay that ferries on its drifts the crows and jealous buzzards that roost on ledges blackened with deathrattle and who come trickling in to drop pieces of its scabs and rain them against the town, rancid heaps and gobbets that no amount of cleaning can get rid of or make becoming to any passers, so that all must continue bathing in the pollution—come to take the dire stink for granted—that in time the custom should salve the wound forgot.

At the moment I am using the thin rope of my belt to hang myself. The moonlight leaking over the curtains and cracking into sharp stars against the black bedroom ceiling while I stay hovering between two nights, as it were, like a man whose feet are straddling the boundaries of territories, feeling the separate tug and pull of armies that are vying to enlist him, that are tearing the gist of his limbs, and he can taste of that new citizenship where he did not know he so fiercely wished to belong.

It is there I can begin to see the faces. They come floating with accusatory stares and go hanging about the purloined air, light and immaterial, gone as quickly as pipe smoke. Such figures flash and disappear, denizens of a dark world, their presence a rule of laws steeped in the very air. Though I have not tried counting them, I know that there must be three hundred and forty-two—even the face of Old Ruckus with its hurt and bashful stare watches me from its thin home among the shadows—each of them met because a devouring is taking place, for they have come to watch Death gorge Himself on my soul.

Crowding me these spectators, they swarm and assail me with the bared teeth of memories from a life no longer mine, all of them licking their lips like hounds eager to taste the blood. In their sniffing, tonguing, and howling, they are helping the wind how they can; they are preparing to stomp me like vermin. I have run out my luck years ago.

For there among the wind a dark light prefigures a spirit. It is the boy set up on the gate. The manner in which he ripples implies he is so much more than his appearance would allow. His dreary flesh and mangled inners become rejuvenated by the breeze from the cave.

He watches me, eye to eye. Each of us held in the other one's image. He is torn, I can tell, between contentment he is dead and longing with all the beats of his stilled heart that for even just a second he wasn't. He has come to steal my last breath. To taste and savor and sing in the chorus with the rest of them:

> *We who were alive but yesterday today are not.*
> *Once you found us laughing,*
> *Then you were there to mourn;*
> *Wherefore life twists and changes like the twitching of legs,*
> *Like eyes buckling from a skull.*

At which point, seeking my lips, he comes and tenderly kisses me, his fingertips grazing my jaw. I can feel the wind

welling up out of me, out of my digestion, out of my stomach, marrow, the veins crashing to a halt: he is drawing the
pith of my soul.

At which point the arm stringing me up drops down
automatic and the belt buckle spins on its graphite lips and
I am vomited down on my bed.

Gasping big banquets of air. My heart struggling as it
kicks and pumps and attempts to rid itself of the boy's frigid
brand. Above me the moonlight pulses over the curtains. I
who have touched the rock of the underworld with the tip
of my outstretched toe, my body once again beginning to
sit taut, can feel my bugged-out eyes making their retreat
to my sockets—these eyes that sting from his fixing stare or
from gazing through him to the shadows, each in his void
giving the illusion of an interminable well.

As I lie here flowered on the bed, incredulous I am truly
awake, something regurgitated from Death's stomach and
too masticated, digested to be of much use, I think about
George Cilton and his swindling me of my breath. How
he saw the boy explode and his partners shoot their exit
and how he must have strode to the corpse, the dark yet
crowded with splintering echoes, and how bending toward
his mouth not yet tepid wafted that final suggestion of life,
a suggestion that should have been mine.

My lungs are searing: they feel the rip of a cat who has
clawed his way out, leaving behind tattered shreds.

I begin to hitch my pants, thread them with that thin
leather hoop by which you can step from Death's bastion to
life and back. I can see George Cilton at ease wherever he
is, sleeping the sleep of peace in that crowded home of his,
well-meaning and knowing he has robbed me of my right.

I am got up onto my legs. They are a little wobbly still from the veins that are knocking and make the blood a sort of whitewater, but even more I can see the whispering beginning to move: it is desperately wishing to reach me, almost crying that it is still too early to be here as soon as it wants, and so I sense the breeze comes crawling at me on its belly like an infant's slow slithering but certain in the struggle it will reach me, reach me one day at last, though whether this is truly the last as it swears it is I do not figure to know.

Following myself as I grab my gun, I find I must confront this wind since the wind is already looking to find me, determined it is to arrive.

16

By now the pain in his eye had rooted deep. The stench festering of unlimed graves, you could smell it across the road and down the street, the terrible scalding from the pith of his brain as if someone had implanted inside his skull a live coal.

He was ordering shots by twos, one to throw back, the other to douse his wound in hope the whiskey would make sterile whatever was continuing to torment him. Half his face looked like he had given it up for dead.

"You pass through Utica these last weeks?"

"I ain't passed through Utica since I had a reason to wag my wick in the wind."

"Well, I weren't there but since two days—you see, they got this old boy there that'll break the spunk out your worst mustang the second he sets switch to rump. You throw him the wildest ridgerunner you can snatch you off the prairie, that'll eat the living biscuit right off your hand, and he'll iron her out flat: she'll be fit for the governor's wife after that old boy gets through with her. But the reason how come I bring it up is when I weren't there but since two days they'd gone and strung this blown-up fella up at the top of their gate. I came in, and there he lay, just sitting up atop there, smiling down, bidding you welcome. You tip your hat and trot on through. Friendly town that Utica."

"Sounds to me like he must've stuck his head some-where where he ain't supposed to. Made him give up his quest."

"Way I hear, he robbed the bank."

"Sounds to me like he robbed a bit more bank than bank."

"Well, whatever he done, it ain't no acceptable existence stringing him up for the kites and sparrows of the field. You'd expect him to lift off the ground any old second, seeing as how he's got so many a wing to him. They got guards standing over him day and night, but they ain't shooting the birds. You should go see yourself, that is, if you can stand the smell. Thing smells like an outhouse laid to waste—like after your mother pays a call."

"Hey, watch it now, Sott. Don't go dragging my mama in, not unless you want a slice of hell yourself."

Outside graveyard quiet. The street and buildings and restive horses powdered with nacreous dark. Quinn was waiting for them, the star in his eye winking from the shadows.

He waited until they were loosing the tethers. Then stumbling forward, pretending he was drunk, but not feigning much since in truth the earth was pitching and rearing . . .

"Say, any you boys spare a quarter?"

"Get lost, fella."

In that instant he dropped the blade. Like a tongue it stuck from his sleeve, and he whirled at the man, tearing a gash from wrist to shoulder.

The next instant the man lay writhing on the ground, but on thinking twice he went abruptly still in a possum play of dead, ever so faintly rocking. The other reached toward his belt.

"Don't," said Quinn and cocked the belly gun.

He let his hand go limp.

"If money's your angle, you'll be sorry to learn I don't own a penny."

Out into the noon of night he stepped, this hideous boy of a cyclops.

"I may not look it to your dumb ass, but I've enough money to heavy god's hand. What I want from you's an apology."

"I'm sorry," said the man. From a distance it looked like two people just talking.

The air began to kick up, the breeze canting their hats, a musty sour within the wind signaling he had already lingered too long.

"You offended my dearest kin, who is worth any five to your dumb ass, worth any ten to your sort, and I'd be grateful if you'd go begging his apology."

"I'm sorry" he was again on the verge of offering when the path of the bullet sprouted amid his brain. A liquidy stem whose petals withered on blossoming.

"Shoot," said Quinn. "How about you tell him yourself."

When they ventured out to see in what arrangement the gunfire had fallen, they found a corpse curled over, the other mute and swaying like something at home in the depths of the sea. He had stolen their horses and was fixing toward Utica.

The next morning in an anonymous village, having spent the night on the steps of the bank, he woke to the teller jingling at him his keys. He shook these in his light in the manner of a witch doctor raining an aspergillum over a baby. Quinn squinted open an eye.

"I'm afraid you'll have to get moving, son. The customers'll be here for nine."

His tired scowl widened to sincere beaming.

"Shoot, hoss, they ain't starting till after I run her through!"

Within the week he was back in Utica after gathering the supplies: a creaky phaeton; a bumpkin's getup that included an unbleached straw hat and eye patch, so that he looked a disoriented pirate mistaking his ragged carriage for a galleon in quest of plunder; and, most importantly, all the bladders, canteens, and casks of whiskey he had been able to get his hands on, the contents of which he had taken and mixed together.

Long before he entered the town the smell had sought and halted him. At first he thought he was kidding himself, for he saw nothing but empty plains. He figured he was going funny from too much travel and the odor the fumes of a mind that had lately become nervous from solitude and that had gone about twinned ever since he could recall. Perhaps the carcass of an animal obscured in brush.

Then he sighted the birds. A congregation of dots peppered the vast gray quilt, their circling as insubstantial as those invisible motes that tag one's vision.

On drawing closer he had no choice save cinch his bandana around his nose. He cursed his mouth for tasting it, for filling his lungs with the stink.

Then he saw it: there against the entablature of the great stone gate lay the corpse strung up like a challenge. His feet and hands were wearing the skin of crusted raw bone, his shaggy visage a terrible grotesque to ward away nightmares, his stomach swollen the obscene width of a fat man's. At first his instinct was to stand up and holler, to gleefully applaud the prank that he had managed to pull off to the amazement of odds. Though by the time his phaeton was passing under the gate, following the weak hello he raised to the band of guards that glared at him over their shrouds, as he recognized the putrid horror to contain the scent of his brother, he was weeping with divine despair.

That evening he tasted the fruits of his wealth. At the tavern he bought round after round for any who found his proximity. Indeed, if he sensed a man were running his gaze against flesh, that lusty hypnotism holding him in place as if under the sway of curves and crevices and beginning the imaginative foreplay, intrigued by what egregious monster should hold beneath, he would summon her over, then, feeding her cleavagesquint with double the amount of fair, would toward her yonder, nodding and shooing her hence, until she reached the covetous stranger, a gift from this emissary of good will. He was not just steeling his courage for what he had to do and treating the celebration as a possible last meal in which he could go out with his spurs singing, but rehearsing the reckless character he would perform for the second act of the night, whose wastrel spirit harbored the only hope he had of winning his twin from outrage.

Although midnight had just chimed when he bid the sparse company farewell, the bar for that hour was unusually peaceful, so many patrons having been treated to their pleasure now fast asleep upstairs. How peaceably they lay, like angels after war!

Outside the few that went about did so under handkerchiefs. A few had clothespins clipped to their noses. Gasping, hacking, choking. The odor rancid beyond villainy, for it besieged all other thought, all other topic of conversation, was all anyone could think or talk about, that or deposing the mad sheriff whose idea it was stringing him up there. The outrage dauntless to the smell.

The closer he got to the gate the more the stench took hold of him. As he neared the pass, it grew unbearable, a noxious, ravenous impudence that consumed all history, clogged all thoughts, deeds, breath, sight, pores until it seemed he himself had become the smell, since there allowed no distinction beyond the putrid flagitiousness but to loathe the smell and despise the smell along with the entire genealogy responsible for bringing about this plague that, thrown into the pit, would prove impossible enough to run out the devils and make of hell a ghost town.

In spite of the trenchant dark he could make out birds by the dozens that should have been in their nests, vying for a perch. Gobbets had dropped from their beaks and pocked the dirt, which resembled an exodus of trod-on snails.

Three guards sat by, looking idle and perturbed. Then just when Quinn heft them a goodbye he let go a rope that as consequent sent down a bladder filled with whiskey, the bloated contents of which went babbling onto the dirt.

"Son of a bitch!" yelled Quinn and whoaed his horse. The guards stood to, but watching him.

He hurled himself from the phaeton. His madcap gestures frantic, furious, controlled. He pinched the neck of the bladder, swearing, showing it to his audience as if he were producing for them a drowned chicken.

"Wasted! All of it! Goddamn whiskey cost me a goddamn fortune! Shoot," he snuffed.

He stomped his boot. Blankly he stared up at the stars while he wondered if he should yell, how long he should wait, the guards watching him just as blankly.

For some moments he fidgeted there before drifting back and hoisting himself on the carriage. Then, about to take up the reins, he let fall another bag. From the ranks of the puncheons a cask lumbered forth and burst on the ground.

This time the guards ran to help, Quinn falling as he scrambled out. They rolled him the broken barrel and showed him the bag, and beholding the company of them standing out there in the miasma, he began to swear in such a way as he had never, even shocking himself by what came gushing out, something inside him having snapped. He was pouring out everything, cries of outrage, cries of joy. He stomped his hat. He tore his hair. He whipped himself on the head as if he were being scourged by hornets. The guards looked on, a little afraid, nonetheless captivated by this man who since his arrival had brought an end to their boredom.

One of them dared to console him. Quinn just shrugged him off, once again resuming his invective against his luck, his luckless trade, the asphyxiating stench of the carcass dangling overhead until he rested truly limp against the wheel, his voice raw from the terrific effort he had summoned for the charade. The earth was drenched with whiskey.

"At least them worms get drunk," said a guard. Quinn pretended to grimace.

"Shoot," said Quinn. "After that feast they been fatting on all day, from what leftovers they getting from them birds, I bet they're right to wash that fella down with a sup of my good whisk."

Now the lot of them broke into laughter, partly from relief at finding his mood had brightened, partly encouraging.

"Shoot, wish I was them worms," said a guard. "You can eat about most anything you care to want, and folks let you alone. And you ain't much rid with no damn nose."

"Wish to hell I was drunk," said another. "I already got me the worm. But I'd say he's more a snake to your worm, Al."

"Say, how much we have to pay to get a sup of that there whisk? You know, take the edge off the damn stink."

"Shoot," Quinn grinned from under his crazy hat (his smile was genuine), "I'll give you boys a nip on the house, seeing as how you saw the worst of me and all. I been riding my broke ass these years, so tonight I'm drinking bottom up."

He took the nearest full canteen.

Soon they took to chatting. They were asking him where it was he was from and how long he had been cooking whiskey and how any fellow could stand to make such a living from such a trade that demanded such stern mastery of himself; for if he should take to cooking whiskey, another rejoined, he should as soon drink up his entire capital within the week, making himself his own best customer and quickly becoming rich off himself while finding, to the contrary, he was addled all the week and indigent.

Then another sprang from his post and commenced to imitate Quinn. He mimed the barrel erupting and the booze filched to waste. They clapped and hooted, whistled. Even Quinn laughed, keen and suppletory, as the guard, emboldened, mocked him further. He was tearing his hair. Staring with his good eyeball. Beating an anguished dirge on his breast. Challenging the Almighty to throw down his scepter and put up his dukes. Hell, he would allow him the first punch.

"I'm sorry," said Quinn. "I . . . well . . . you know. I know sometimes I get awful bad. I weren't that bad, though, boys, was I?"

"You sure was swollen up."

"Bout as cheery as a pissed-on ant."

"Shoot, I downright thank you for putting up with such a sorry some bitch as myself. I do feel bad, showing you all my mean side. Would standing a second drink undertake to bury the hatchet?"

"Shoot, we might even let that little hissy fit slide and take to liking you."

"I just hate to be the reason you boys get in trouble."

"You just trouble yourself about getting us more of that whiskey."

After they passed out, he flung off the hat and eye patch and started the climb up the gate. Kidding himself he was soberer than he was. Forbidding his glance below. It surprised him that the act required no superhuman amount of strength. He could keep on going, continue climbing, so far as saving should need.

On reaching the height of his brother, he held there for a spell as if fear or fatigue had finally caught up with him. Gripping the stone for several seconds. A sloth clinging for dear life as he sleeps. He had not seen him face to face for the longest while. Amid those obsidian wrecks of plumage nestled from top to toe, he slumped as he had in life, in some sullen pose of mourning or despair. In that manner he beheld his brother and also a grim prefiguring of the selfsame rot.

"Shoot," he murmured. Then he remembered the knife.

He wedged out the knife from his backpocket, and praying that no one would pass and that he would be gone with the corpse in moments, he began to saw at the rope. The act demanding a fearlessness akin to persistence. Which soon began to fray, then break—then snap!

The body speeding the height down and the flock of birds scattering, but not so startled they did not immediately drift to where they had been.

Quinn rushing them, yelling, shooing. He had to curb himself from shooting them each.

Before taking the corpse to the carriage, he studied it: the manner in which he lay, had collapsed on the ground, the leisurely torsion, though assuredly dead, still retained a posture of being alive. He had seen him thus when he was resting from a hard day's run, so that he told himself he would not be surprised at all if Irving, the fall having knocked him to breath, should move with a faint pulse of air, suddenly displace his arms and pushing himself erect remark the stint abroad.

He went and took the blanket and cast it over him and carried him to the phaeton, spew threatening to disgorge. Carrion eying him for the slippery thief he was. He stowed the body between the barrels. While he did this he realized he would have to bury him fast since anyone with a nose would be able to scent his whereabouts within a mile and could track him based on the smell alone.

Preparing to abscond, he glanced at the pile of guards. Their snoring the only sound for miles apart from the stomping of his horse. He could not resist the idea of playing some kind of joke, some jest in his brother's honor, and he ran to where they slept, the sheer levity of the prospect making him chuckle out loud.

Standing there, resolving the final kinks from his merry prank and grinning, regardless of the hour, a bullet entered him from the nape, cleaving his teeth and cheek with a great gap, nor having registered the gun's explosion. Rather, balancing for a second, his shadow appeared to hang in insensible currents before he collapsed on the dirt.

After a while Les emerged and strode carefully to the body. All three guards were fast asleep. The thief had fallen on his stomach and he waited without movement. Only his blood crept toward his boots.

To watch him, he seemed in the thrall of a thousand commitments. At one moment he would heft and sight the gun, taking clear aim; at the next he would jerk it down and reign the gun at his thigh; then he would bend and squat on his heels, perhaps preparing to inspect the corpse or turn him over, but then he would hastily rise up, glancing this way and that and peeking over his shoulder perhaps to see if anyone were watching. He had the panic of a child who is afraid to pick up a snake and who, even though he has cut off its head, continues to fear some harm. It was obvious he could not choose whatever he wanted to do.

After a while he fired: a bullet into his skull burst his left ear. He had eight shots remaining. Then after the four he knew he was going to quit firing before he set about doing it. There was gruel and bone and brainmatter, a wet corolla about his head.

With his boot he wrenched him over and fired a final shot into his face, which had become all but unrecognizable. In the attitude of an auctioneer inspecting a reasonable wheeler, he beheld a fault in one eye.

The guards were woken, George roused from his bed and ushered to the scene. He conducted him about, explaining how this deed had led to these—it had stayed just like he'd left, the horse and buggy and corpse right where they had been—a weary George blinking as if at once to waft away and welcome the stuff in Les's story, his expression that of horror and bland expectation suggesting he had gone from the thick of a bloody dream to a world whose terrors were no less dreary.

"You really had to shoot him that much in the face?"

"I shot him once on the stand, no, twice. Then when I came over, he startled me when he jerked."

A black bloodprint had dried and pooled where the felon rested. In the air a sterile hint of alcohol.

"You knew he would come, and come he did. And I suspect folks'll get to thanking you just as soon as they get through with setting fire to their clothes." He said this in that wry tone he had of being a trifle cross. He was peering at Les with a sense of nervous wonder.

But Les was ignoring him. Rather, he was staring at the body that, though it remained beside their toes, his frown declaimed had somehow still escaped him.

"Guess I'll go on and bury those boys."

17

When he saw Utica borne out of the dark—the roofs and walls the size of a thumbnail, an excrescence on the edge of sky that throbbed with each step of Irving's horse, a hovering prefiguration of doom or justice or some kind of value to the elusive nature of things—it came as a sad relief.

For the last several months he had looked at the surrounding countryside, where he had seen trees of different types and hills of different contours that leaned into different skies along with different farms and cabins, surroundings that, for all their variety, appeared much like those he had known growing up, and the effect of wandering through these sights had again led him to confirm that almost everyone across the nation must be but a slender variation of everyone else, that, though he had once been taught to know there were fundamental disparities between a Yankee and a Rebel, had viewed the cities, homes, and cane fields drying after a thunderstorm as items essentially Rebel, which themselves had spawned a manner of thinking distinctly antagonistic to his own, both were far more alike than he had given them credit. He had come to realize that both in their blind rabid hatred of the other had been obstructed from seeing the truth: that in fact each was defending the other and that through the murder of their own they were protecting an enemy who was themselves, that in fact war was a tangled love. North and South, he had come to perceive, retained far more in common than they meant to accede, each at bottom having the exact core desires, so that they maneuvered less as opposites than they worked the same gray realm, the snap of a trigger a loving embrace.

For the last several months, in passing farm after farm, and every one of them exuding a determined lassitude and lust to keep aloof—the cloistered pastures and ascetic shingles like squalid hermits that had forsaken the world for a private illusion—he saw only the false perimeters through which he could expect to perceive the demarcations of eternal brotherhood. Every person he met on his travels, whether man or woman or child, ignorant or schooled, malicious or benevolent, upright or crouched intently, was merely a variant, these minute and simple disparities the helpful petitions for the soul to start from its self-satisfied slumber and venture to forge the bridge on which he could welcome this obscure friend, embrace him with open arms.

Yet of late the rule had changed. No longer did he see them as marks on a curtailed spectrum that he was happy to collapse like a network of paper dolls by means of fraternal love; now he was willing to recognize that some from the very start were severed from that network and rendered things apart—these were plotting the others' downfall and had to be stopped by the good at all costs. Furthermore, it was not how they all aligned but that they were plummeting headlong to vast and certain destruction, and staving this off for as long as possible was the collective single aim.

Still conceding that the war had produced a futile tendency to categorize as North or South, as Right or Wrong, as Yes or No, he was beginning to espouse a new faith tempered by fierce pragmatism: that there were some egregious qualities and some base people that remained beyond the grasp of hope and for whom love was a disservice, a corroborating of that villainy, people intent on hastening the common ruin, their perverse growths the fulcrums around which they had bent and warped and that no amount of hammering could hope to smooth and that in the interest of the greater good demanded being cut down.

He understood that, with his typical ingenuity, he had hidden this important caveat from himself, indeed had somehow even known it all along. It had taken the hard wisdom of these last weeks to trace the wickedness that had served to wreck his life. Each thread, he now saw, went back entire to Gruhn—if he was acting, it was a reacting against it, Gruhn; if he was cognizant of an abhorrent thought, in it he recognized Gruhn—so that truly he perceived if there was any real hope of sundering himself from that part he was keen to destroy, then it meant damning himself when he extirpated it along with the one that had borne it. Not until he had found her confirming his worst fears did he fathom the depths to which the enemy had ruined not just him and his brothers but had mutilated his mother to the core. Gruhn had broken and warped her, had dislodged her and made her something useful for his purpose alone, some purpose that remained out of sight. As far as he was concerned, the woman she had been was over; he had gone there with the intention of rescuing her but without ever thinking that the person he might rescue he was rendering more lost.

For all the day she said nothing. He waited; her small, frail hold on him scarcely touching him, he waited until he forgot. Casting back to ensure she was still asaddle.

He tried asking her about the years he'd missed, first by telling her stories from his life as a schoolteacher out East, as if hoping that by observing the fluency of his tongue hers might take to mimicking and shade the outline that he had only begun to trace, but these attempts to induce her to admit what Gruhn had devised, the contours of his craft, were, like a dandelion's petals dispersed by an infant's breath, met with no resistance, so defenseless she was her defenselessness seemed protection, his words obliterating her silence to idiocy.

She was no longer his mother, this husk of a person of someone he used to feed from. No atom of soul. All integument, no kernel.

Yet if this vague presence magnified his hatred against Gruhn, it foiled his plan of whisking her away and ensconcing them somewhere where he could account for her and spend the future making good on the loss. Now and then he noticed himself working out how he might get rid of her and in such a manner as without incurring the guilt. Her presence tagging him and gloomy and compelling his mind to dwell on evil thoughts, she became the embodiment of his failure to come home, his disappointed prize. Fair she was and gentle when in hope he had begun the journey, and now he was shocked to catch himself debating about snuffing her in the night, justifying it by saying that if he were of such an age and mind he would pray a friend could decipher his pleas from his aspect of senile gloss and be yet merciful.

He was trying to figure out the right manner of doing it—leave her on the steps of a charity home or pay a poor family the expense of caring for her—but as soon as he found himself tangled in this sort of wrenched speculation he abruptly halted it, insisted she was his to bear and his alone—remorse, regret, discomfort, everything—as part of the penitence for his neglect and the wickedness he'd effected, as part of the reshaping that was to mold him into a good man, a man the opposite of Gruhn.

Silence lay on the town, though long before entering it a stench had wafted over the plains. That acrid rot of flesh decaying. He had not smelled it in many years: the scent of a turned-up field. Not thick and stultifying as he recalled, and that could humble regiments to their knees, but this at first light and almost fragrant, the sweet stink of summer milk gone spoiled and poured to the dogs. Would it have been thus had he returned to those same fields months later, and, apart from the scars of cannonwheels and the muddy paths of bivouacs, the tracks frozen in their hurry, apart from the craters of shells and ruins of trees and barns, he could almost begin to kid himself that what had happened never had?

Gradually, as they drew closer, the odor grew worse, and he perceived the circling carrion, their wheels empty of a carcass.

People looked at him, seemed to know his secret. He tried to think how they could, if anyone could pair his face with the crime, and sifting his brain, he found he had made no fatal misstep, had left no piece of evidence overlooked that would yield him up, something as damning as a personalized photograph. The only mischance he could construe was if somehow Quinn had been caught and, describing his kin in detail, urged them to be on the lookout for the one-armed lefty with whom he had promised to reconnoiter—then he could see he was sunk. In the meantime he had to verify with what stealth he could whether the authorities lay in wait.

They took lodgings at the first tavern, the kind of place no man before had ever entered at the flank of his mother, nor would he have were he not banking on being gone by night.

Using the change from one of his ingots, he paid the cost of the cheapest room and ushered her upstairs.

"We have to bury him, Eddie. He ain't had no funeral to keep him in."

"I know, Mother. I'm about to see about that. For now I need you to get some rest. We'll be heading back out this evening."

He lay on the far edge of a bed tainted with copulation. After a while he tipped forward his hat so that it shielded the gray morning light, his anxiety, his suspicion beginning to subside like the guilt of a bad crime.

Was this not what he had wanted? Coming home to an empty house where the fire of life was she, ready to be whisked away to a haven where he could happily requite her for the years spent without returning a word, the simple cloister where her maternal air would ensure he would never wander again from his principles, the two of them greeting each morning with an optimism and moral certainty that the philosophic life bred as a consequence.

On her side of the bed he heard her muttering.

"Don't go anywhere, Mother," he said, and soon he fell asleep.

When he woke he had the vicious doubloon of noon in his eyes. His hat had dropped to the floor. To his side his mother lay asleep on her back. Her snoring pocked the air, her breath coming masculine, indecent, vulgar.

He retrieved his hat from where it had fallen, and he watched her splayed there on the bed. Her mouth agog, her thin, pale tongue hung limply on the perch of her lip like something he was not supposed to see, like a private part that had lost its taboo significance and succumbed to the same plainness inherent to the hardened palms and brutish shoulders and sun-browned face destroyed in its nest of wrinkles.

He watched her splayed on the bed, her legs spread slavishly, and the pose struck him as obscene. He tiptoed to the door, careful not to wake her.

Downstairs the person that had lent him the room was hovering about the bar. Already there were a few drinkers, bearded loners turned to scarecrows through the liquid decades.

"I'm going out," he told the bartender. "Would you mind keeping an eye out for my mother on the chance she should come down? I don't want her to leave since she might get lost in town."

The bartender continued polishing glasses. He wondered if he had spoken loudly enough. Then right as he was about to leave, dismissing the bartender as a strange case of intermittent deafness, the man looked up and met him.

"I got enough business of my own needs watching."

It took him a moment until he gathered the nerve to respond.

"Yeah," he said, "but see, I can pay you. All you have to do is tell her not to go out the front door. Just tell her to go to the room. She'll listen to you. That's all."

"I told you," said the bartender. "Wherever you're going, you bring her along yourself."

"Yeah, but that's just it. She ain't so young she can stand on her feet all day. She's just a little old lady. Now I don't want to keep you and go getting in the midst of your business, but I'm willing to remunerate you amply." He was about to take out his coins.

"Boy," said the bartender, "you don't know when to quit. You keep on going, you're liable make me punishing."

"Fine," he sighed, at this point wanting to rid himself of the prig but also wanting a kind of victory. "Can you at least pour me a damn whiskey?"

He took his drink to a table in the corner. There he sloughed his jacket and undid his sleeve, which he rolled up past the nubbin, letting the skin that had been tucked away these days feel fresh air.

As he took sips of the whiskey he studied the castrated arm. Plump and humanoid, it looked like a piglet born of a second. A weird creature without head or legs. Some monster that didn't even need putting out of its misery. If he closed his eyes and imagined, he could almost entertain the idea that the arm extended to its former reach—his imagination straining, pretending—could begin to sense the branching of a hand into fingers and the fingers into fingertips, those attenuate, deft workers that used to curl and grip and flex and intertwine themselves on their partner.

When he opened his eyes the world was waiting for him in the shape of his mangled nubbin. It was staring at him like an impotent sausage, an annoying presence that cannot be batted away.

"Hiddy" came a lilt.

Against his chest he clutched his stump. She was looking down at him from her lofty, fallen height, a vermillioned lady on her rounds.

"You mind if I take a seat?"

"I was getting ready to leave. Hey, yeah, sit."

He let go his nub and began folding the sleeve, but in such a way and meeting her gaze as to distract her, that he could have been tackling any habitual effort.

"Golly, mister," the woman exclaimed. "Who done that job, a drunken butcher?"

"You haven't happened to notice a certain fella come in? He'd've had an ugly mess of a black eye. A bit of a sorry sight he'd envisaged."

Sensing her hesitation, he promptly qualified it with: "I can make it worth your while." And he laid ten dollars on the table. Each successive coin ringing her greater interest.

"Say, I ain't gonna get busted just from associating with you, hoss?"

"Why would you?"

She swept the money into her gown, clearing the space between them save the table's spectral gloss that held their shady undersides.

"That guy, he came in last week. Fogging up the place with that awful stinkeye and buying screws for any folks who walked through the door. More than could keep a good carpenter's hands full. But since then he's been right killed."

"Killed? What? When?"

Some slumped heads lifted, and she glared for him to hush.

"What happened?" he shouted at the edge of a whisper.

"Sheriff Les done hung that other one up who robbed the bank." He could hear her fingering the coins. "Hung him up on the gate, laying him up for the buzzards of the field and to catch whoever it was that was helping him clean out that safe."

"You saw him hang?" said Edward.

"No, he ain't ever hung up that other fella. Sheriff Les shot him when he come back trying to collect his partner—what was left of him, I'd say."

"And he didn't think to hold him none? To find out where the gold he said he'd stolen was? He didn't think to, like, interrogate him at all?"

"Honey, not that I heard tell. I think the way Sheriff Les done figured, it was someone had to pay in some way more than metal, and he expected his soul could best chip in."

"Damn," said Edward. "Just shot him down dead," and he made a motion with his arm.

"It ain't no surprise," she added, as if offended by his innocence of the matter. "Don't you know the law ain't much for fretting these days, otherwise we'd be run out of town?"

"Shoot," he said. But that was all he could think to say.

He stood. He was about to push in the chair, but then he stopped. He clipped a few more dollars on the table, her winsome puppyish pout suggesting he might stay.

"Say, you wouldn't know where any of that gold is, would you, mister?" Her tone something of a dare.

"I wouldn't know where boo is."

"You was just asking to ask."

"That's right," he glared. "Just asking to ask."

He was on the verge of going but turned back again.

"If I can request a simple favor. Would you kindly mind keeping a lookout for an old lady who might come down the stairs? She's sharing an upstairs room with me. Just stay her if she aims to head out."

Shock blossomed across her face despite the cake of rouge and kept her in the chair.

"You're the one that brought in his mama!" There was judgment in her voice. "Boy, you're crazier than I thought." Her look said it was less admiration than revulsion that caused her to show a smile of assorted teeth.

"Keep an eye out for her, will you? She's not right in the head."

She was staring at him without blinking and in such a manner that expressed she did not believe such a person could stand before her.

Finally she jerked toward him in her chair. "With three crazy sons, you can bet your cherry cracker I'm gonna be aiming to set her free!"

18

Once she woke, her instinct was to seek the window. Yet angled as it was, the window contained only the stern blank stare of sky, so she got out of the bed and stood against it where she had a ready command of the street.

How long she remained there looking down—pedestrians eddying among currents of wagons, horses by themselves and in groups—did not concern her or seem to register. Little in that view must have encroached on her awareness. The attitude in which she watched them come and go resembled a chore that, if she failed to execute, could arouse very serious consequences.

Tensed, she stayed there at the sill, fiddling with her hands, trying to make it appear she was satisfying the task to her utmost capacity . . . until she saw the thing go past. Although she had never seen him before in the daylight, she accepted his advent without question.

Without delay, as if incited by fear or fervor, she was driven forth from the room. Down the stairs, out the door, onto the busy street, to follow him as she had.

Strange noises stabbed the harsh bright air; still she held true, went unaffected (the charged hoofbeats and alien chatter at any other season ganging together for the sake of cowering her to an impotent wreck). Temerarious, intent, she continued seeking this figure whose familiar will, even from a distance, she could decipher in spite of his featureless aspect.

Though he never turned or glanced as he was wont, she could perceive from the arch of his back that he had become far deader than dead, as if corpses could die once more. And it was then she understood why he was hovering in plain day: he was searching for his love. Lost to his nightly element on account of his diminishing form, he was looking for her to restore him. For her skin to warm and compass him and balk him from wandering. And it was now she made the discovery: she saw she could overtake him!

At first she thought it an accident, some mishap of her vision or some trouble in length and distance. Then, as she began to gain step by step, she understood it for no wrong but the demand of his accord. He wanted her to touch him; he had allowed it to happen. Her legs would have stayed frozen were it not for the unbearable urge with which he chastised her to come.

Along the street they went, his form taking on larger just paces beyond, weening to actuality, summoning her to his chest, while her keen steps continued in the expectation of merging herself on him. Growing from yonder to nearly there.

Not once did he look back. So sure he must have been of her devotion. Pleased she knew how to work his command. Pleased she was pleased to perform it so.

When they turned from the road, she lagged scarcely a stone's throw behind him. A great welling of joy or fright, which perhaps for her had become one and the same, as she beheld him enter their house and welcome her from the curtains, and eager to show she had grown his will to hers so succinctly, thrilled that he had summoned her with the object of drawing her close, she slipped quietly in behind.

19

In she goes. The sounds his waiting at what he wants. Inside amongst his things, his chirps and jitters yelling her on.

Fearful if she moves he is to fade. For it is of a kindly and a true. To take him to her arms, his stay a-holding and afull, the linen dripping blood.

She hastens but so's not to frighten. She feels the faith a-beckoning to enter, his chirps and jitters yelling her with love. Through his den the warmth of skin wanting there and waiting and eyeless stare shorn with hate, wanting his bidding moved. She feels him hovering there, adrift yet staid. It is of a long sad quiet hunger that only the pain of a body can know. She knows you, dear as wife to husband.

Beyond the door there comes a weeping. A telling of her to come. In leading her this way he knows she's good to work his will, to catch him in her arms and bear him at the verge and nurse him on her blood. So fair she is and young, and ready in hope to begin the journey, the welcome-back loving-clinging and the offering of blood.

Open the door, round the bend. She hears his chirps and jitters. The pain of allowing his must, since in the day he ain't to rest, but of night he ain't to sleep, only the waiting and the quiet and wanting him to come.

The skin cuts smooth, easy as a knife to butter and as kindly for to peel the cover off an unburst bud. She tears this piece, knowing you to smile, alike her in her gift, and in taking so to stay. Then another, happy for how the skin gives to demand. A queen before a feast, since any pain is joy, and the more for him to take, the more there is stay, the weight for him to come.

She gathers so much she can, ready to take you here in arms, for she can sense the blood soak to a sponge, like minnows in the sun, fleeing her embrace. There ain't no drifting, no waiting, no yonder, but ahead he stays, dear love compan. He is still of body and naked. His flesh a solid kind of thing, his figure in dark bloom, and so I cast it on him of a kindly, knowing him to stay.

We two go looking face to face. His sightless eyes, whose stare they are, hollow no more and flutter: they are two bulbs opening for the first time, babes of a first day, and it takes a spell for him to halt, to see she is for good. The two of them reading the depths of mind, dear as wife to husband.

The flesh to quit his drifting, has made my figure for a name, since, the wishful joining, in placing a finger on the face that seals our touch, I tell him what he has hollered for me to speak:

"Les Tamplin," I say.

20

On quitting the trammeling dark he thought he noticed a glint of disappointment to Irving's horse, who appeared to be searching him for all the bullion he had failed to exhume.

He had been unable to return to the gold. There were precipices that, scramble as he might, required company to raise him. With only himself and his good arm, he began to perceive it was impossible to surmount the barriers he had earlier passed over when his brothers stood by or jump the chasms without extinguishing himself or the flame.

Eventually, after what seemed like hours of straining against edifices that had previously taken a half minute to scale, of almost dropping and breaking the lantern and banging his head against rocks, on reaching a slab that no amount of maneuvering or ingenuity save another person's hand could see him reach the top without welcoming the fact that he would slip and be maimed, alone in the broken dark, he decided to turn back.

While he hurried the route back to town he tried sifting his memory for some trustworthy friend whom he could take into his confidence, someone who would be willing to drop whatever employment he had at the moment in order to follow him to the cave, where maybe the tote had already been reclaimed, someone who, if it were there, would not devise to kill him the second he saw the gold, but no one came to mind.

Moreover, he considered bypassing Utica and forgoing his filial duty and riding until he encountered that friend.

He reminded himself of the oaf who alights on a saddled mare, thinking he has stumbled across the best luck of his days and that after a few simple fixes he will gain a nice fortune, and only once he has sunk his savings in trainers and veterinarians fathoms the beast is worth more dead than alive, yet for all the expense of readying it saleable has clenched shut the trap that makes him believe there is still a great profit to be had. To be unlike such a fool, he strove for the means that would allow him to rid himself of her without the guilt. Yet nothing for his purpose seemed suitable—there was abandoning her and nothing else—and he could not leave her behind since he knew how his conscience would haunt him, try as he might to ignore it.

In his worst of fantasies he thought about why he could not guide her to the middle of a quiet dale and end her before she grasped his intention, despite his telling himself that were he so witless and aged, from inside the cage of his lunacy, he would hope some kind acquaintance or relative would have the charity to do him in—nor could he thrust her back on Gruhn. All he could do was surrender himself to approving the difficult presence that testified to his innate dumb idiocy to make things right or wait for the ordering principle that governed men's lives and implanted in them feelings like love and remorse and beauty to note this and intervene.

On nearing the town he was puzzled to hear at this late hour a subdued din at the bottom of the night. As if a battle were taking place several miles away. A distant murmur came like a rustling of reeds or like the twitching and shivering of winter leaves when there is that desperate clinging to what has been, a will to keep fighting the inevitable fall.

As he cautiously approached he saw, rising up through the dark, a stringent light from the town center. The rumble now pitched to a swarm of voices, among which he could hear deliberate shouts.

Paralyzed, for fear the mob tipped to his robbery had staked the town and was gathered to welcome him with lynching, he held there on his saddle, motionless, were it not for his horse that continued to jog.

Drawing near the square, he saw the whole town ablaze in candles, lamps, lanterns, torches, which rendered it a ghastly noon of night. Hundreds of people had turned out and were flooding the square, so many they must have come from nearby towns. Families, children, widows on horseback, afoot, in wagons, they had all turned out for the spectacle and were whorled around the far end of the square like a thwarted maelstrom that seethed against its bright center wherein a makeshift gallows had been erected and was guarded by tiers of smoldering torches. From his saddle Edward fumbled out and cocked the Remington.

What he could see from even this distance was a man nude from top to toe being led to the noose's cavity, his body tallied with scars. The crowd burst into shouts and jeers when it perceived him mounting the steps, a storm of furious cries and curses thrown up at his dignified gait as if the felon had demanded they should meet this way and this way only.

Regardless of the distance, he beheld he was no stranger. He tethered his horse and hurriedly set about fighting to get toward the platform.

"Wait!" he shouted. "Hold it!" Which was swallowed in the crowded air.

His wrists had been bound, and a dour official was fixing the noose around his throat. Nothing about his figure suggested he was resistant. Until now his eyes had been locked just a few steps beyond where he stood, but perhaps courage or curiosity made him seek the mob, scanning them as you would the weather. Still stoic and resolved despite the rope that cinched his neck.

"Wait!" cried Edward. "Please don't kill him! Wait!" His shouting lost in the furious calls only added to the uproar.

He whipped a path toward the front where the man lay hovering before him on the scaffold. Though he had not seen him in fifteen years, here he was beyond containment.

He followed his stare, and his breath was stopped by what he saw: there, like a defect of sight, he recognized his mother. The woman that he beheld was a hideous monster whose whole body had been transformed to a bloody gown. She lay there among attending feet, her ears and nose and lips shorn off as had much of the skin from her face and breast. Several matrons from the crowd were weeping and beating the air and screaming out for this man's end. Nonetheless her eyes kept locked on his. Her mouth, or what remained of it, he could read, was gibbering over and over his name.

When he turned back the rope had tautened and he was dangling in the sight of the crowd. A great cheer surged, a commotion of joy and wrath.

The hanged man's gaze, which had popped from the grip of his skull, still continued on Annora as if announcing for her aloud: Yes, this is just; this is right.

"Cut him down!" he shouted, but his voice only added to the uproar of the mob.

Then casting back at Annora, he beheld she was dead. The two sharp points that peered out from her sordid mask had softened, stuck to their grip on Les. Then turning back once more, he saw him, still alive if barely, his finishing body turning to a tight point as it grew from dying to dead, fixing on her yet, a sense of determined approval through the last of his wobbling and heaving while he beheld her haunting stare.

It was in that manner he last saw them.

Then he turned and ran.

21

Asaddle he woke, adrift like the stuff of memory. Gathering himself, he turned and squinted behind him, but there was no one seeking him, only plains and more plains more. His horse loping, he took the reins from where they'd fallen, fighting to slow them to a walk, and continued in the direction the horse had set.

On the horizon clouds were bleeding out, and once the sun rose they went lifeless, the horse persisting and Edward sensing he should tighten the reins, if only he could fix on a direction.

He cast around, wondering what else there should be: an honest woman, a just and good vocation, some other gold waiting for his taking. (If he only turned them slightly, the opening of some new future, himself the fixed point of a compass around which flourished so many petals, every fraction of a coordinate surrounding him and the horse a million different Edwards, each ripe with its particular inanities and inanitions, just sitting there, waiting to emerge.) The horse picked up of its own accord, and he allowed it to lead him on.

Several days passed, and a great storm settled atop them. Lightning cutting the ground while he fought the horse to walk.

Then one day he woke to find the rain and clouds had disappeared. Dawn had enlightened the sky and the hills behind him, and it rose fundamentally incongruous with the dark skies he had come to expect for so long.

As he palmed handfuls of creekwater over himself, he watched the steam smoking from the Appaloosa. The mist in which it moved. Curious and unusual in how the cloud hovered around the leather. The horse a sudden phantom of itself, yet calm as any guide, fearless and wholly other.

As he began to piece together what had happened, he saw all events as branching from their sole mover, and the only mover there was, of course, was Gruhn. It was Gruhn who had trained the twins to steal and to hate and to violence. From any angle you could recognize it, Gruhn. Gruhn moving, a worm curdling the milk of the true, Gruhn plotting to effect some downfall; it was just like Les had told him time after time after time. To accept it would be an affront. Everything that had worked their ruin followed because of Gruhn. From the beginning he had made it his life to undermine them. Actions had resulted from, barricades had been sidled by, confrontations had served to embolden him.

He had nearly reached it when he saw where they had been heading all this time. So many miles and now to be here, pawing the ground. He could not but smile to think he would have ended at any place else. Patting Irving's horse with bewildered approval. Whether he had trained the thing to aim that way unwitting or if they had returned by instinct alone he could not say. Only that he had come home to bury Gruhn.